MURDER IN PALM SPRINGS

A High Desert Cozy Mystery - Book 8

BY

DIANNE HARMAN

Published by: Dianne Harman
www.dianneharman.com

Interior, cover design and website by
Vivek Rajan

ISBN: 9781093535235

CONTENTS

ACKNOWLEDGMENTS

Palm Springs is iconic. Blue skies, golf complexes, and the most beautiful sunsets in the world. No wonder so many people choose to spend time there. I so appreciate all of you who have opened your homes to me over the years and told me your stories. This book is loosely based on one of those stories.

My thanks to Michelle, Mike, Lamine, Noelle, Jacqueline, Ray, Pam, John, Shirley, and Bob, for being so supportive of my success as an author. I'm honored to have you as friends. And especially to Tom, who recently arranged a surprise party in recognition of my success. It was a fabulous night, and I thank you all!

And to each of you who have read my books, taken the time to contact me, and given me your input, please know how very much it's appreciated. Readers, none of this would have been possible without you. Thank you!

Win FREE Paperbacks every week!

Go to www.dianneharman.com/freepaperback.html and get your FREE copies of Dianne's books and favorite recipes immediately by signing up for her newsletter.

Once you've signed up for her newsletter you're eligible to win three paperbacks. One lucky winner is picked every week. Hurry before the offer ends!

CHAPTER ONE

The little bell above the door dinged as Marty opened the door of The Olde Antique Shoppe, a Palm Springs institution owned by her friend, Carl Mitchell. Danica, his assistant, looked up from the display she was arranging and said, "Carl's in his office. I'll tell him you're here."

"Thanks, Danica. I'll look around and see what new treasures you two have added since the last time I was in here," Marty said as her eyes swept the walls and tables of the small shop. She spotted a white jacket studded with gold and walked over to it.

Marty was reading the information card on the wall next to it when Carl walked over to her and said, "Pretty amazing, don't you think? One of my clients bought it at an auction years ago, and he's quite ill. He's trying to get rid of as much as he can so his son and daughter won't be saddled with getting rid of everything in his estate. He had a fascination with Elvis Presley and that's why he bought the jacket. As you can see from the information next to it, the jacket belonged to Elvis. Believe me, I thoroughly checked it out, and it's the real deal."

"I think I recall seeing pictures of him in that jacket. That's quite a coup, Carl. Given the older population in Palm Springs and the wealth here, I'd think you should be able to easily sell it."

"As a matter of fact, I've got a guy in mind that I'm pretty sure will want to buy it. Does the name Jimmy Joseph ring a bell with you?"

"It sure does. By coincidence, I got a call from him this morning and that's the main reason I'm here today. You know my sister's boss, Dick, sends a lot of business to me. Jimmy wanted to insure his rock star memorabilia collection, but he had no idea what it was worth, so Dick recommended me to do an appraisal of it.

"I'm great on silver, china, furniture, and things of that nature, but I've never appraised celebrity memorabilia. I came by to see if you'd like to help me do it. You're far more knowledgeable in that area than I am."

"The answer is absolutely yes. Small world, but I'm going to be seeing Jimmy play tonight. After his heart attack a few months ago, his doctor put the kibosh on him traveling. He used to headline in Las Vegas and other places all over the United State, but no more.

"He loves to perform and when Mark Saltzman, he's the owner of the Red Velvet Lounge, found out Jimmy's doctor had told him he couldn't travel anymore because of his heart condition, he asked if Jimmy would like to perform at his place once a week. Jimmy's doctor gave him the go-ahead, and I have tickets to see him tonight.

"He's a huge collector of music memorabilia, and I thought this jacket would really appeal to him. I'm hoping to have a chance to tell him about it after the show. When are you scheduled to do the appraisal?"

"Tomorrow, can I count on you?"

"Marty, I've got to be honest with you. Murder is just not my thing, and it seems like every time I help you on an appraisal, somehow someone ends up dead. That or I have to come in contact with your sister, which scares the heck out of me. Every time I think about how she whacked that Styrofoam wig stand in half with a butcher knife and pulled out a missing diamond ring, I get the willies.

If you can assure me neither one of those things are going to happen, I'm all in."

"I can definitely tell you that Laura has nothing to do with this appraisal. As far as murder goes, you're going to see the man tonight, so I think I can safely assure you that murder is out of the question."

Sometimes it's better not to make assurances, as Marty was about to find out.

CHAPTER TWO

Eve Wright picked up her ringing cell phone and looked at the screen. *Swell,* she thought, *just what I need. Another bail me out call from Mickey.*

"Yes, Mickey. What's new?"

"Gosh, Mom, you make it sound like I'm committing a crime when I call you."

"Trust me, Mickey, the only reason I sound like that is because that's usually the only time I ever get a call from my son. When he's committed a crime, needs bail money because he's in jail, or needs money to pay someone back before they commit a crime by killing him for the money he owes them."

"Mom, you're making it sound like I'm a real loser."

Eve didn't say anything for several long moments, hoping he got it – that she did think her only child was a loser. Then she said, "What is it this time, Mickey?"

"Mom, it wasn't my fault."

"You sound just like that loser father of yours before he ran off and left us. Nothing was ever his fault either, particularly the part about when his boss found out he'd been embezzling money from the tow company where he worked. So, what isn't your fault this time?"

"Mom, it's like this. I was walking through one of the casinos here in Las Vegas on my way to a job interview. I'd heard there was an opening for a bartender. Anyway, I saw an old friend of mine, and he asked me to have a drink with him. He told me there was a Pai Gow game table at the casino that was so hot you couldn't lose at it. He'd been playing for two hours and was up $100,000. He was afraid his luck would change if he went back to the table. Said it was a shame, though, because that table was golden. I thought about it for a couple of minutes and told him if he'd loan me the $100,000, I'd pay him 50% interest, and I'd go win money at that table."

"Mickey, tell me this is some nightmare you had and it really didn't happen, because I think I know where it's going."

"Mom, it was a sure thing. My friend said there was no way I could lose."

"You lost, didn't you?" Eve asked.

"Well, not right away. See, for a while I was sitting sweet. For a long time, I had a stack of thousand-dollar chips in front of me, and then I started losing. I wound up losing all of it. My friend stayed in the bar so he wouldn't jinx me. Guess it didn't matter. He could tell by the look on my face when I returned what had happened. I didn't even have enough money to buy a drink."

"What did your friend say about you losing it all?"

"What could he say? I told him I'd pay him back."

"And how do you intend to do that?"

"Mom, I know you're not happy with me, but if you could loan me the money, I'll pay you back."

She laughed. "Right, just like all the other times. Well, Mickey, afraid you're out of luck this time. I don't have any more money to give you. I sold the house the last time you did something like this and there is no more money. I can barely make ends meet as it is. I'm down to a pair of jeans and a tee shirt. It's a good thing the restaurant provides us with uniforms or I wouldn't even be able to work, because I sure can't afford clothes, and quite frankly, riding the bus, because I sold my car to help you, doesn't make me feel real successful. Sorry, Son, I'm afraid you're out of luck this time."

"Mom," Mickey said, his voice suddenly sounding terrified, "this happened a week ago. I don't think my friend believes that I can pay him back. Last night two men came to my front door. They had tattoos all over them, shaved heads, and bodies that looked like they must work out in a gym all day. That or they got those muscles in prison. Mom, they told me they were going to kill me if I didn't come up with the $150,000 within ten days. They said they'd be watching me all the time, so I better not try to leave Las Vegas."

"They told you they were going to kill you?"

"Yeah. Mom, I've been thinking. I know you and Uncle Jimmy don't speak because he hated Dad and thought that was the reason your mother died. Because you broke her heart. Maybe enough time has gone by that he'd forgive you. He's so rich, what would $150,000 be to him? He'd never miss it. Why don't you call him and ask? If that doesn't work, I'll be dead next week. I have nowhere else to go to get the money."

Eve was quiet and then she said, "All right, Mickey. I'll call Jimmy, but this is the last time I will ever try to help you. Do you understand? This is it. From here on out, you're completely on your own. I'll call him and let you know what he says."

"Thanks, Mom, you're the best. I'll be waiting for your call. I really don't want to start looking at urns or caskets just yet."

"Mickey, I don't want you to either. Goodbye."

Eve paced back and forth in her small apartment and wished she had a cigarette. Even though she'd given them up twenty-five years ago, right now she craved one. Several years earlier she'd worked at the telephone company for a short time. She'd been hired on a temporary basis and it hadn't turned into a permanent position, but the one positive thing she'd been able to do was get her brother's unlisted phone number.

She went to the kitchen drawer that served as her office in her small studio apartment and rifled through the papers in it until she found what she was looking for, Jimmy's unlisted home number in Palm Springs. She punched in the numbers on her cell phone.

The woman on the other end of the phone said, "Joseph residence. May I help ya'?"

"Ruby, this is Eve Wright, Jimmy's sister. It's quite important that I speak to him. Is he there?"

"I'll check and see. Be back in a moment."

Several minutes went by and then the unmistakable sound of Jimmy's voice came over the phone. "Lawdy, lawdy, Eve. Been a long time. Understand ya' need to talk to me."

"Hi, Jimmy. Thanks for taking my call, and yes it has been a long time. I know we've had our differences in the past, and although I'll never believe that my marriage caused Mom's death, you and Mom were right about Charlie. He turned out to be everything you said he was. Left me high and dry and embezzled from his company. I divorced him several years ago."

"I'm jes' sorry ya' didn't find out earlier. That's a lotta' time to waste. And your son, Mickey? How's he doin' these days?"

"Not so good. Seems like he's got a lot of his father in him. As a matter of fact, that's why I'm calling. He's in a little trouble, and I could use your help."

"What kind of help, Eve?" he said, his voice suddenly much cooler than it had been.

She took a deep breath and told him about Mickey's gambling, the amount of money he owed, and that his life was being threatened. She told him she'd spent every penny she had on Mickey's past problems and was living from paycheck to paycheck just to keep a roof over her head and food in the pantry.

"Jimmy, I'm begging. Please help me. They're going to kill my son if he doesn't pay the money. I know you told me once many years ago that you didn't approve of the man I married, but that you still felt obligated to leave something in your trust for me. Please let me have that money now, rather than when you're dead. It will save your nephew's life."

It was very quiet on the other end of the phone and then Jimmy spoke. "Eve, I'm sorry for you and Mickey, but this is a result of his actions. I'm not givin' ya' any money. Same thing'll jes' happen again. Ya' know it, and I know it. If somethin' happens to Mickey, so be it. I'll keep ya' in my trust cuz' you're probably gonna' need that money at some point fer you, not fer that no-good son of yers'. Ain't spendin' the money I worked so hard fer on some deadbeat gambler. Nice talkin' to ya', Eve. So long."

And with that, the connection was severed. Eve stood for several moments looking at the phone in her hand, not sure what to do next. She knew Mickey was waiting for her call, but she also knew the call she'd just finished effectively sealed her son's fate. She had nowhere else to go.

She pressed the phone number for Mickey into her cell phone. He answered it immediately. "Well, Mom, did you get it? Is Uncle Jimmy going to give me the money?"

Eve sighed deeply and said, "No, Mickey, he's not," and then she went on to tell him what Jimmy had said.

Mickey never hesitated. "Mom, guess that tells you something.

He's got the money for me, but the only way I can get it is if he's dead."

"No, Mickey, that's not quite true. The only way I will get money is when Jimmy dies. From what I understood him to say, there is no provision for you in his trust."

"Mom, get serious. You know if you inherit some money from Uncle Jimmy, and I'm in a jam, you'll help me. I know you will because I'm your only child and you love me. So saying, it's pretty clear what has to happen."

"I'm not following you, Mickey."

"Mom, you don't have to do anything. I'll take care of all the dirty work. Let's put it this way. From what I read in the papers, Uncle Jimmy is living on borrowed time ever since his ticker had that big problem. If he was to go out a little early, rather doubt anyone would suspect it wasn't just a natural thing."

"Mickey, I don't think I like what you're saying."

"Mom, trust me. You don't have to worry about a thing. I recently read that dear old Uncle Jimmy walks out to his mailbox every day at the same time for a little exercise. The article even gave the time, ll:21 a.m., every day. According to the article I read, you could set your clock by it. Now if somebody was driving by and something happened while he was out there, it would be a sad thing. But then again, you'd get your inheritance, and I'd get my life saved."

"Mickey, you live in Las Vegas, not Palm Springs, where Jimmy and I live."

"Yeah, Mom, but by the miracle of the modern age, I can do a one day turnaround. Four hours there. Five minutes for what I have to do, and four hours back. Piece of cake and then all my troubles will be over. I'll call you in a couple of days and you might want to spruce yourself up for the reading of the trust, if they even do that anymore. Gotta go, Mom. Lots to do. Talk to you later," Mickey said as he ended the call.

Eve sat in her chair contemplating everything that had happened in the last hour and finally smiled. *Maybe it is time for that sanctimonious brother of mine to see if the heaven Mom always talked about really exists*, she thought.

CHAPTER THREE

Miles Reed walked out of the Red Velvet Lounge, totally frustrated. *Yeah, Jimmy Joseph is good, but so am I,* he thought. *Half the people who were there tonight were the same people who came to see me when I used to play at the Velvet. Only thing the guy has going for him is his celebrity status – a washed-up, over-the-hill, guy with a bad ticker.*

Miles walked to his car. He knew he was as good a singer and piano player as Jimmy, and Mark Saltzman, the owner of the Red Velvet Lounge, agreed with him. The meeting he'd had with Mark prior to Jimmy's performance had not gone well. The problem, according to Mark, was that Jimmy had a following that guaranteed sold out performances every week. Miles didn't as yet have a drawing power that strong, and according to Mark, if he did develop one, it was probably a few years away.

It wasn't just his ego that had been damaged. His bank account had taken a severe hit when Mark had let him go several weeks earlier so he could hire Jimmy Joseph. Miles knew he had a loyal following, but it was pretty small compared to Jimmy's. He thought a good compromise and a way to keep his bank account in the black was to play at the Velvet on some other night of the week. That way Mark would have two good revenue nights a week.

Unfortunately, Mark hadn't seen it that way. He felt if he had live entertainment two nights a week it would cut into the profits he made off of Jimmy. The reason being that it would dilute the exclusivity of Jimmy's shows, and he could charge a lot more for Jimmy's shows than he could for Miles' shows. And that had been the end of that.

Miles had gotten jobs playing the piano and singing at a couple of other clubs in the Palm Springs area, but they weren't just a step below the Red Velvet Lounge, they were a staircase below it. If you performed at the Red Velvet, you were someone. If you performed at any of the other nameless clubs in the area, you were just another down-on-his-luck musician, a nobody.

Miles was a Zen Buddhist and had always practiced non-violence. Mahatma Gandhi, the leader of the Indian independence movement, who had been successful in achieving self-rule for India, was his idol. Miles was so opposed to violence that he even took spiders outside to free them rather than squash them. The only reason he'd chosen to become a Zen Buddhist rather than follow on Gandhi's path was because there was a Zen temple just a couple of blocks away from his apartment, and he felt Zen and Gandhi's philosophies were pretty much the same.

A couple of his musician friends commiserated with him and said that since Jimmy had suffered a major heart attack, maybe he'd have another one, and then Miles could star at the Red Velvet Lounge again. However, being such a strong believer in non-violence, he couldn't justify wishing that Jimmy would die.

Miles had become consumed with Jimmy Joseph. He read everything he could find that had been written about him. He'd even found out where Jimmy lived and had driven by there more times than he cared to count. Miles had never met Jimmy, but he'd seen him walk out to his mailbox several times as he drove by Jimmy's estate.

Miles preferred to think that what he was doing was not stalking Jimmy, but some would say that being consumed enough by someone to drive by their home almost daily could qualify as stalking.

Tired, discouraged, and nearly broke, Miles walked into his small house and felt more depressed than he'd ever been. He fixed a vegetarian stir fry, sat down on the couch, and turned on the television, aimlessly surfing through channels, when something caught his attention.

The host of the show, the Poison Chronicles, was talking about a Bulgarian dissident, Georgi Markov, who was exiled and lived in London in the 1970's. In 1978 he was waiting for a bus near Waterloo Bridge when he felt a stinging pain on the back of his right thigh. He looked around and the only thing he saw was a man bending down to pick up his umbrella. He thought nothing of it at the time, but he soon developed a high fever and died three days later.

An autopsy revealed a tiny pellet the size of a pinhead in Markov's thigh. The pellet contained a small amount of ricin, a deadly poison. There was speculation that the pellet had been fired from an air gun hidden in the umbrella.

The host said that Markov had mentioned the man with the umbrella to the doctor when he was admitted to the hospital, but if that was the man who poisoned him, he escaped. The host had then gone on to talk about the poison, ricin, and how it was obtained from the beans of the castor bean plant, which is a very common plant. The host mentioned that laws regulating the production and use of ricin were very difficult to enforce, because it was so common.

Miles was interrupted from watching the rest of the show by his phone ringing. It was his brother calling to see how his meeting with the owner of the Red Velvet Lounge had gone. Miles told him the owner had made it very clear that Jimmy Joseph would be starring at the Red Velvet Lounge as long as his health permitted, and he was not going to hire Miles to play another night.

His brother, Danny, had said all the appropriate things such as how unfair life was and sometimes you just get dealt a bad hand. Then he went on to say that if it was him, he'd just get rid of Jimmy.

"Miles, I know you don't believe in violence, but look at it this way. Jimmy's landing path is pretty short about now, meaning he's living on borrowed time. That heart attack just about did him in, and with a little help, seems to me it wouldn't be too hard to make him permanently go away. With him gone, you'd be back in business. Think about it. If you decide to do anything, let me know and I'll help."

Miles had ended the call, horrified at what his brother was suggesting, but at 3:00 a.m., after another sleepless night, he began to think there might be some merit in using ricin to get rid of Jimmy. After all, everyone knew Jimmy went out to his mail box at a certain time. Someone could easily drive by at the moment Jimmy was at his mail box, deliver the ricin via an air rifle, and be in one of Palms Springs' adjoining cities in a matter of minutes.

When the idea occurred to him, he was horrified that his mind could even conceive of such a plan. After all, he'd been a practitioner and proponent of non-violence for a couple of decades. Then he heard a little voice in the back of his brain say, "Miles, this isn't about non-violence. This is about survival of the fittest."

Troubled, Miles finally fell asleep.

CHAPTER FOUR

Marty walked into the courtyard of the communal living area she and her husband, Jeff, a Palm Spring police detective, shared with her sister, Laura, Les, a well-known artist and Laura's significant other, and John, the owner of the very successful Red Pony food trucks.

"Morning, Laura, everyone take off as early as Jeff did this morning?" Marty asked.

She sat down at the large wooden table where they shared their evening meals prepared by John while he used them as very willing guinea pigs for different recipes he was testing for his food trucks and catering business.

"Les is sleeping. He told me his personal art muse was very busy with him at the moment, and he probably wouldn't see much of me for the next couple of days."

"I've heard of muses for writing, but I've never heard of one for art. Does Les have a name for his?"

"He told me it's kind of one of those 'If I tell you I'll have to kill you' things. Says he has no idea where his art comes from, and that he has a name he calls his muse, but it's never to be spoken."

"Sounds kind of strange to me," Marty said.

"I agree, but given the fact he has a waiting list for his paintings, and the amount of money he charges for each one he sells, who am I to tell him his muse is a figment of his imagination?"

"True," Marty said reaching down to pet Duke, her black Labrador, and Patron, her white boxer, who shared Laura's psychic ability. Sometimes the two of them scared her with their ability to sense things that were going to happen in the future, but when both Jeff and Marty's lives had been saved because of that ability, Marty had stopped doubting, and now she paid close attention to it.

"I saw Jeff when he left," Laura said. "He told me he expected to be busy for the next couple of weeks with the big concerts coming to the desert. He said he just hoped the kids left it at drugs and alcohol, and that there wouldn't be any homicides. Jeff felt the detectives in his department had enough to do with the routine things that went on in Palm Springs."

"Yes, I remember when we helped John with his food truck at the three-day concert a couple of years ago and we ended up solving a murder. I'm sure Jeff doesn't want a repeat of that. Speaking of John, how is he? It seems he's just getting busier and busier," Marty said.

"He is. I was out here early this morning having coffee and answering emails when Max came in to help him get things ready for the day. They packed up the food trucks and John mentioned they had a catering event this evening, but he'd made a beef stew for us and all we had to do was reheat it. He told me to be sure and serve it with the soda bread he was leaving on the counter for us."

"Sounds great. That should help me make it through the day. Honest, that guy's cooking is totally spoiling me. If anything ever happens to him and I have to cook for Jeff, he might leave me. We neglected to put the word 'cook' in our marriage vows."

Laura laughed and said, "If he does ever leave, we'll all probably be put into the Betty Ford Center to help cure us of our addiction to his food, but fortunately he seems happy here."

"How could he not be? He has four adults who eagerly await whatever he's going to serve. He lives up here away from the traffic and plasticity of Palm Springs, he's doing what he loves, and he doesn't have to answer to anyone. That's kind of everyone's dream," Marty said.

"To change the subject. What's on your agenda today? Dick mentioned something about you doing an appraisal for that rock star, Jimmy Joseph," Laura said

"I am. I thought I needed a little help with it, because I've never done a music memorabilia appraisal before, so I asked Carl to help me."

"That was probably smart. I guess some collectors pay huge amounts of money for celebrity's things. I'll be curious about what you find. Tell Carl I said hi."

"Actually, I think I'll pass. The mere mention of your name sends him into a cold sweat. I honestly don't think he'll ever recover from the wig stand event."

"Speaking of which, Marty…"

"Don't even think about it, Laura. I can see from that look in your eyes you're going to say something I don't want to hear." She put her hands over her ears and said, "Na na na na na na na," like a child who was trying to keep out bad news.

Just then Patron began to growl as he backed up to Marty's leg and pressed against her. Marty took her hands away from her ears, looked at Laura and said, "Okay give it to me straight out. Looks like Patron has picked up on your vibes, and while I don't like to be in this position, I suppose you better tell me what you're sensing."

"Sorry, Sis, but I have no choice. There's going to be another murder, and unfortunately, I think you'll be involved. I just want to give you and Carl a heads up."

Marty was quiet for a few moments and then said, "Because you included Carl in this, does that mean it has something to do with the appraisal we're going to do today?"

"You know I can only tell you what I'm given, and I don't know the answer to that, but I think Patron does."

As soon as Laura had started talking, Patron had resumed growling and the hair all along his back was standing on end. "Laura, I have to go, and we know from past experience, when Patron starts acting like this, it's hard for me to get away. Would you talk whatever mumbo-jumbo he understands and calm him down, so I can leave?"

"Sorry, Marty, no can do. I'm getting a message that Patron needs to go with you today, and no, I have absolutely no idea why. You better take him."

"This is just swell. I'm going to call Jeff. Maybe Jimmy Joseph was murdered last night or something." She picked up her cell phone and pressed in Jeff's number.

A moment later his deep voice said, "Hi, love. I let you sleep in. How are you doing?"

"I'm fine, just wondering if you've heard about anything happening to Jimmy Joseph. I was getting ready to pick up Carl and go to our appraisal, but if something's happened to him, I'll need to make other arrangements."

There was silence on the other end of the line for several moments. "Marty, I have no idea what the devil you're talking about. I've heard nothing about Jimmy Joseph lately other than it's almost impossible to get tickets to his weekly show and that you're doing an appraisal for him. Why do you ask?"

"Because Laura has some murder premonition and I can't stop Patron from growling, plus now Laura says I need to take him with me to the appraisal."

Jeff was quiet for a few moments and then said, "If nothing else is certain in life, Laura's premonitions are. Take Patron with you. Do you want me to send one of my men to his house and he can stay there during the appraisal?"

"Absolutely, emphatically, no. I mean, I should walk in and say, "Oh hello Mr. Joseph. I've brought my psychic dog with me and this is officer whoever. I brought them with me because my sister had a death premonition and my husband insisted I have them with me. That would definitely put poor Carl right over the edge," she said.

"Yeah, you probably have a point. Okay, let's compromise. I won't send an officer over there if you promise me you'll take Patron with you. Tell Carl and Jimmy Joseph that your husband insists you have a guard dog with you when you're appraising things that are highly valuable. Tell him it also provides protection for him."

"All right, Jeff. You and Laura win. I am definitely not happy about this, but I'll take Patron with me. See you tonight. Even if you are over-protective of me, I love you." She ended the call and said, "Patron, we've got an appraisal to do. So long, Laura."

"Marty, I see a mailbox. Be careful."

"Swell, Laura, just swell. Like I'll only pass a gazillion of them on my way to Jimmy Joseph's house. Am I supposed to look down every street to see if I can find one without a mailbox?" she asked sarcastically.

"Mark my words," Laura said enigmatically.

CHAPTER FIVE

Carla McIntyre walked out on her veranda and couldn't help but look at the palm trees on the other side of the white stucco fence, the fence that separated her spacious yard from Jimmy Joseph's yard.

She'd done a lot of research on what she considered to be an abomination against the natural beauty of the desert. A lot of people thought that palm trees were perfect for the Palm Springs area, and Carla agreed. It wasn't that she didn't like palm trees, she did. She thought the small ones were beautiful, but not the ones she was looking at.

The five palm trees in Jimmy's back yard, flanking his pool, were Mexican Fan Palms, a species that reached one hundred feet, and she was sure his were approaching that height.

She hated that the first thing her guests noticed when they stepped into her back yard wasn't the infinity pool she'd spent a fortune on, or the carefully landscaped yard filled with rare drought-resistant plants, or even the beauty of the San Jacinto Mountains her house backed up to. No, the first thing anyone noticed were the ugly palm trees in Jimmy Joseph's back yard.

Carla had talked to her attorney about suing Jimmy and getting them removed, but he'd suggested that instead she talk to Jimmy about the trees. First of all, lawsuits could get expensive, particularly when wealthy entertainers were involved. Second, having the trees removed after an amicable discussion would be a far better way to handle the problem when neighbors were involved.

Her attorney had even quoted the Robert Frost poem, Mending Wall, to her which ended with the words, "Good fences make good neighbors." When he'd finished reciting parts of the poem to her, he told her he'd had to memorize the poem for a college English class, and he'd never been able to use it for anything. And finally, after all these years, he'd had a reason – to save her the cost of a lawsuit.

Several times when Carla had been returning home or going somewhere, she'd noticed that Jimmy Joseph always walked down his long driveway to get the daily mail in the mailbox just outside of his iron gates. It was the only time she ever saw his gates open.

After her conversation with her attorney, she decided to meet Jimmy at his mailbox the following day. That morning, she dressed carefully in her Palm Springs best, because even though they were neighbors, Carla having moved into her home only a year ago, she had never met the legendary Jimmy Joseph.

She carefully picked out a cream colored short-sleeved silk blouse and paired it with silk slacks. She took the large diamond ring she'd inherited from her mother out of her jewelry safe as well as the one carat diamond earrings that had been a gift from her ex-husband.

The earrings gift she now knew was a "guilt money gift," hoping she'd refrain from posting on YouTube the embarrassing photographs which had become an overnight sensation on social media. Having a high-profile husband was not always a good thing unless you were able to get a hefty divorce settlement, which she had.

Carla looked at herself in the full-length mirror in the dressing area of her bedroom suite and thought she looked exactly how a former movie star should look when she went to meet her famous neighbor. Elegantly casual was the look she was going for, and she thought she'd nailed it.

Her short blond hair feathered around her heart-shaped face made her look like one of the legions of wealthy ex-wives living in Palm Springs. Unfortunately, although her face was charming when she'd played ingénue roles, it wasn't quite the look movie producers wanted for middle-aged women, and thus her current title of "former movie star."

Carla had often thought the mailman, whose name she'd learned over the last year was Geoffrey, must have some type of syndrome which caused him to deliver the mail at the exact same moment every day. Not a minute earlier. Not a minute later. At 11:42 a.m. each day her mail was delivered. On this particular day she opened her gates and walked down the driveway to get her mail.

She saw Geoffrey out of the corner of her eye as he put the mail in the mailbox of her neighbor to her right. She turned to the left and walked down the street to where Jimmy Joseph's mailbox was located. She decided that Jimmy Joseph must have the same syndrome as Geoffrey, for true to his character, he was only a few feet from his mailbox when Carla walked over to it.

"Hi, Mr. Joseph, I'm Carla McIntire, your next-door neighbor. We've never met, but I often see you getting your mail when I drive by, and I thought it was time for me to introduce myself."

"Nice to meet ya', ma'am," Jimmy said, extending his hand. "Welcome to the neighborhood."

"Thank you, and I do love this neighborhood. Backing up to the mountains and being a bit away from the hustle and bustle of Palm Springs is divine. Have you lived here very long?"

"Yeah. This has been my base for over thirty years. Matter of fact, when I bought the land, there weren't a thing on it. Had help, but purty much had a hand in everything that was built and planted here," he said in a proud tone of voice.

"Even those huge palm trees by the fence?" Carla asked. "They're about the biggest I've ever seen."

"Yeah, ain't they jes' somethin'? I think they're jes' about the prettiest things in my yard. Their little green heads up against that blue sky. Man o' man, jes' don't get much better than that."

"I'm surprised to hear that coming from someone who obviously loves beautiful things. I'm told that you have a memorabilia collection that is incredible, but I must say that those Mexican Fan Palm trees are really ugly. I mean, they just go up and up and there's this little tuft of green at the top. Unfortunately, they're the first thing my guests notice when they walk out on my veranda. I was wondering if you might consider cutting them down? I'd even pay to have it done."

"Are ya' crazy?" Jimmy asked. "When I planted them little trees they was jes' babies an' look at 'em now. Brings a smile to my face every time I look outside."

"Mr. Joseph, I hate to say this, but they're an eyesore. Your property would be so much prettier if they were gone."

"Ain't gonna happen Ms. McIntyre. Them trees will be there until the day I die, so ya' better get used to 'em. Y'all have a nice day, ya' hear?" Jimmy said as he abruptly turned around and walked back up his driveway.

Carla turned around, walked to her mailbox, and took the mail out of it. *So I have to look at those awful trees until the day he dies. I hear he's got a bad heart. Just might happen a little sooner than he thinks. No one tells Carla McIntyre something isn't going to happen. Carla McIntyre always gets what she wants*, she thought.

Maybe Jimmy should talk to my ex-husband. My ex-husband never found out that I was the one who arranged for those photographs to be taken. I knew he was having an affair, and I also knew that was how I could get the money that I could live very, very well on for the rest of my life. This really shouldn't be all that hard, I just need to figure out the best way to do it.

CHAPTER SIX

Carl was standing in front of his shop when Marty turned the corner and stopped in front of him. She pushed the passenger window down and said, "You can put your appraisal gear in the trunk. I popped it for you."

A moment later he opened the passenger door and looked inside. "Uh, Marty, why is Patron in the car?" he asked as got in and closed the door.

"You know what a worrier Jeff is. Somebody told him that memorabilia items can get really expensive and given that Jimmy Joseph is right up there with Elvis Presley and Elton John, he thought we may be appraising some pretty pricey things," she said brightly, omitting the part about Patron growling earlier and his hackles being raised.

He looked over at her and asked, "Did Laura have anything to do with this?" Before answering his question, she quickly pulled away from the curb, afraid he might try to get out of the car if she remained parked in front of his store.

"No," she said mentally crossing her fingers. "Just bringing a little insurance. I'm not expecting any problems," she said as they passed a mailbox and inwardly, she groaned. *What had Laura meant about mailboxes?* she wondered.

"Good. I've had enough of those for a while. Anyway, I'm really looking forward to this appraisal. I think I told you I had tickets to see Jimmy at the Red Velvet Lounge last night, and he was amazing. I can see why people used to wait in line forever to get tickets to his shows when he was in Vegas. It really was one of the highlights of my life."

"Did you have a chance to talk to him about the Elvis jacket?"

"I sent him a note before the show, and he sent one back asking me to come to his dressing room after the show, which I did. I had a picture of the jacket with me. I thought it would be tacky to take it with me, anyway, he's very interested and I brought it with me today. He told me to set a couple of days aside for the appraisal of his collection, because he has it all in a separate house on his property, if you can believe that."

"Dick mentioned something about it, but he was having a hard time believing that someone could have a memorabilia collection that would be big enough to fill a house. Usually people just have an item or two from some celebrity that they follow. I guess Jimmy's collection is pretty unique."

"I have to tell you, Marty, to be appraising the collection of a living legend is pretty heavy stuff. Hope I don't hyperventilate and pass out or something."

"That's why I always bring smelling salts with me on appraisals," Marty said.

Carl looked over at her and saw that she was grinning. "You're kidding, right?"

"Yes, Carl, I'm kidding. Looks like that's his mansion up ahead on the right. Good thing the gates are open, because I don't have a code to get in."

She entered the palm tree lined driveway and involuntarily shuddered as she passed a white stucco mailbox whose design matched the large house that was Jimmy Joseph's. She came to a stop in the large circular driveway in front of the house. *Was that the mailbox Laura had warned me about?* she wondered privately, not wanting to alarm Carl.

Marty and Carl took their appraisal equipment out of the trunk of the car and walked through the courtyard and walked up to the double doors of the house. The grounds of the house were spotless. There wasn't a leaf out of place.

Marty pressed the doorbell and a few moments later the door was opened by Jimmy Joseph.

"Welcome, welcome. So glad y'all could come today. See ya' brought a dog with you. Is he friendly?"

"Very. My husband is a detective with the Palm Springs Police Department, and he likes me to bring Patron with me as a little insurance when I'm appraising high end items. He wants to make sure that having a collection appraised doesn't make some criminal think it's an opportunity to commit a robbery. Patron is here to make sure that doesn't happen. I hope you don't mind, but Patron will just sleep in a corner and be no trouble at all."

"Fine by me. I like dogs, jes' never felt I could justify havin' one when I was on the road so much. Now that my heart doctor has me confined to Palm Springs, jes' might be the time fer me to get one."

He held his hand out for Patron to sniff, and when Patron had accepted him, he scratched him behind his ears, then he straightened up and looked at Marty and Carl.

"Can't wait to show you my treasures. What ya' gonna' be seein' is the reason I've worked so hard all these years. Dependin' on what kinda' prices ya' gonna' put on the stuff, I may jes' donate all of it to the Palm Springs Museum, although I've had museums from all the States tryin' to get my collection. Don't have nobody to leave it to. I got a sister I'm estranged from and a nephew who's a no-good. Don't wanna' leave it to either one of 'em. Might as well leave it to the museum so lotsa' people'll get to enjoy it as much as I have."

Jimmy Joseph was exactly what Marty had expected from the research she'd done on him. He was dressed in white pants, a white shirt, and a lightweight white jacket. He wore a red silk scarf around his neck which matched the red silk handkerchief peeping out of his shirt pocket.

The tabloids had mentioned that he'd never lost his Southern heritage and certainly, his speech confirmed that. They'd also mentioned, a bit cattily, Marty had thought, that he was a bit too old to have dark brown hair without a trace of grey and a year-round tan. One magazine had commented that it was a well-known fact that the salon he frequented also had a tanning room, the inference being that both his hair and the tan were fake.

Marty looked around the room in disbelief. She'd read in the tabloids that Jimmy's home was white on the outside and the inside was a color reversal. The walls were painted bright red with white moldings.

Every piece of furniture was white, both wooden and upholstered. The accent colors were the paintings on the walls and various types of crystal and gold objects on the tables. It was simply mind-boggling opulence. She glanced over at Carl and could see that his eyes were as wide as she felt hers were.

"Carl, last night ya' tol' me about a jacket you had at yer' shop. Did'ja bring it?" Jimmy asked.

"Yes, I did. Here, let me get it out of my briefcase," Carl said. He opened his bulky briefcase and carefully took the wrapped jacket out and handed it to Jimmy. Jimmy unwrapped it and held it out in front of him and then reversed it, looking at the back.

"I'll take it, boy. It looks great," Jimmy said. "Looks like an Elvis original, and it'll make a durned nice addition to my collection. C'mon, might as well show ya' where y'all are gonna' be workin' the next few days. My personal assistant, Ruby, is waitin' fer us. She purty much takes care of my collection and arranges everythin'. Anyway, I got it all stored in a special house I had built at the back of the property, right past my recordin' studio. Let's go."

A recording studio? A special house for his collection? This is a far cry from where I grew up in the Midwest, Marty thought as she, Carl, and Patron followed Jimmy out of his house and past the pool. On her left, Marty saw a building that she assumed, from the piano she could see through the window, was Jimmy's recording studio.

She remembered reading about a conversation Ernest Hemingway and F. Scott Fitzgerald once had regarding money and how the rich are different from you and me or something like that. It had always stuck in her mind because she thought those two men probably had been rich, but right now she knew Jimmy Joseph was really rich, and he was probably a lot different from her.

CHAPTER SEVEN

Priscilla Simpson entered the Red Velvet Lounge after paying her admittance fee and pinched herself. She couldn't believe that her idol, Jimmy Joseph, was now playing in the Red Velvet Lounge once a week. She'd never felt she could justify spending the money to go to Las Vegas to see him when he was performing there, but she'd read every article that had ever been written about him.

She was a spinster, because she was in love with Jimmy, although some might uncharitably say that it wasn't her love for Jimmy that caused her to be a spinster, it was because no man had ever even asked her for a date, much less proposed to her. She couldn't even be called unattractive. The only word for Priscilla Simpson was ugly, and no man had ever looked far enough below the exterior to see if there was gold there. She had no people skills, and when she did have to interact with people, she was abrasive to the point of being rude.

The internet age and being able to work at home with a computer was a gift for someone like Priscilla. She spent her days searching the internet for anything and everything about the people whose names the insurance company sent her to research before they agreed to insure them.

Her pay was a notch above minimum wage, certainly not enough to ever pay for a trip to Las Vegas to see her idol, and she had stubbornly refused to touch the trust fund her parents had left her.

She felt the reason she had no life, so to speak, was because of the poor job they'd done raising her. To her the trust fund was guilt money, pure and simple.

The show Jimmy put on was everything she'd ever dreamed about. Hearing and seeing Jimmy in person was her Best Night Ever. Halfway through his performance, she thought the only thing that could make it better would be if she could get Jimmy's autograph.

Priscilla carefully took the cocktail napkin that had Jimmy's picture on it in her purse and put it between the pages of a notebook she always carried in her purse, insuring that it wouldn't get folded. She took a business card out of her purse and wrote a note on it, asking to see Jimmy when his show was over. She signed it, "Your Adoring Fan."

When Jimmy took a break, she gave her business card to a cocktail waitress and asked her if she would give the card to Jimmy, slipping the waitress a $20 bill at the same time. She knew she'd probably have to eat ramen noodles the rest of the month, but she'd willingly make the sacrifice if she could get Jimmy's autograph.

After the show she was too excited to stay in her seat waiting for a word from Jimmy or one of his people. She made her way to the door he'd walked through when his performance was over. It was ajar and when she reached it, she heard the words that tore her heart apart, "Boss, some woman wants your autograph, but she's so ugly you shouldn't waste your time with her, and when I say ugly, I do mean ugly."

"Ya' know I got me a limited amount of strength cuz' of this dang heart condition of mine, so if ya' think I should pass, I will," Jimmy said.

"Anyone whose as ugly as this broad probably has just as ugly a personality. I'd take a pass, Boss. You don't need the stress of dealing with someone like that."

"Yer' right. I do need to reserve my strength. Would ya' find her and tell her I won't be able to see her, but thank her for comin' tonight?"

Priscilla never heard Jimmy's assistant say, "Sure thing, Boss." She walked out through a side door with the word EXIT written in big red letters. Tears streamed down her face as she walked the three blocks to where her car was parked. Valet parking was not an option for an ugly woman with no money.

She didn't remember driving home. She didn't remember changing her clothes. She didn't remember getting into her bed and crying herself to sleep. What she did remember was her dream. A dream that was so vivid it felt like it had been real. She laid in bed a long time after she woke up the next morning, and when she finally got up, she vowed to make the dream come true. Jimmy Joseph would have to pay for ignoring her, and as her dream had been very clear about how he would have to pay, all she had to do was follow the directions so clearly laid out in it.

Priscilla may have been ugly, but having her idol destroy her dreams by not wanting to waste his energy on an ugly person, in her mind was beyond cruel and unforgiveable. All she had to do was get on the internet and find the poison that had clearly been marked "ricin" in her dream.

CHAPTER EIGHT

Jimmy opened the door of a large building which looked exactly like his house, only it was a smaller version of it. Inside, it was quite different. The walls were white which showed off items pieces in his collection which had been mounted on the walls.

There were eight or ten rooms in the building and each one had a collection theme, such as clothing, records, autographs, musical instruments, etc. Marty knew from the research she'd done that celebrity memorabilia sold for huge amounts at auction. As they walked through the building, and she saw familiar names, she thought this might be one of the most important memorabilia collections ever assembled, to say nothing of its worth.

A slight African-American woman about Jimmy's age walked through a door and said, "Welcome y'all. I'm Ruby. Been with Jimmy since he got his first gig and lawdy, what a ride it's been. Who woulda' thought when he started out all them years ago he'd have sumthin' like this?" she asked as she made a broad sweeping gesture with her hand.

She continued, "Doc says Jimmy needs to rest a lot and while I know he'd like to tell ya' personally how he got everyone of these here treasures, ain't gonna' happen. He's gotta' get his beauty rest, and I tol' Doc Griffin I'd make sure he did, and durned if I won't, right Jimmy?" Ruby said, shaking her finger at him. "I'll carry on from here. Ya' jes' go back to the big house and take yerself' a little nap. Ya' had a late night and ya' know how Doc frowns on that. Won't tell him how late if'n ya' take your rest now."

Jimmy looked at her threateningly, but it was easy to see this was just a game to both of them. He saluted, and as he was walking out the door he said, "Y'all got any questions, jes' ask Ruby. She knows everythin'. I'll be back later."

When he was out of earshot, she said, "Jimmy's a wonderful man, but stubborn as a mule. Think Doc Griffin knows that and that's why he wants me to go to every doctor's appointment with Jimmy. Guess he's afraid Jimmy'd lie about what the doc said he could and couldn't do."

"How is his health?" Marty asked. "I read in one of the magazines that his heart attack was quite serious."

"Yeah, that's true. It was touch and go fer a while, but that stubborn ol' mule came back. He jes' can't do everythin' he used to do. Matter-of-fact, doc said his health has been, think the word he used was compromised, which bottom line means 'bout the only thing he can do is get outta' bed and go play at the Red Velvet once a week. Takes him a couple of days to recover after them gigs, but Doc Griffin decided if he took everythin' away from Jimmy, might jes' as well kill him. Jimmy lives for the stage."

"Well, he certainly hides it well. He looks like the picture of health, and his show last night was one of the best things I've ever seen," Carl said.

"Glad to hear that. Horace, that's my brother and Jimmy's, guess you'd call him right-hand man, gets him spiffed up every day and makes sure no one sees him lookin' other than like the star he was. Kinda' sad to see the change in him, not as if anyone else would notice."

"You said your brother? Both you and your brother work for him?" Marty asked.

"Yeah, ya' see we all grew up together. My mother lived in Jimmy's parent's house and was his nanny. Horace and I lived there too, so the three of us were always together. His younger sister lived there too, but she wouldn't have anything to do with us.

"When Jimmy got his first gig, Horace drove him, and I made sure he had everythin' he needed. Jes' kept getting' more and more complicated the more gigs he got. Ended up travelin' all over the world. Jimmy's always taken real good care of us."

"Somehow I have the feeling you've taken pretty good care of Jimmy in return," Marty said.

"Yeah, ya' might say that. We jes' one big happy family tryin' to keep one of us alive. Let me walk ya' through the rooms and give ya' a little overall background on Jimmy's collection."

"Ruby, I just had a thought. Since you know so much about Jimmy's collection, you could probably save us a lot of time on research and Jimmy a lot of money. Why don't you show us around and then Carl and I will split up, take pictures of the items, write down the information regarding each item, like what each item is, etcetera, and take the measurements.

"I'll have the woman I use for my appraisals put Carl's and my information in appraisal form, and we'll get it to you. You can go through it and add whatever information you feel is relevant. That way, you won't have to stay with us every minute."

"That'd be mighty nice of ya'. Don't like to say too much, but I purty much need to be with Jimmy all the time, both Horace and I do. He don't wanna' let people know jes' how bad off he is. Other than goin' out to the mailbox every day, cuz' doc says he needs a little exercise, and his weekly gig at the Red Velvet, he purty much stays on the couch or in bed. Ain't got the strength of an ant, but he sure don't want anyone knowin' 'bout that."

After Ruby had given them a brief tour, she walked over to the front door and said, "I'll be in the main house if y'all need anything.

Jes' pick up the bell that's right here next to the door, and I'll be with ya' in a coupla' minutes."

After Ruby left, Marty and Carl looked at each other for a moment. "Carl, I'll start in this room and you start in another one. Let's reconnoiter when we each finish our rooms, but I have a feeling that's not going to happen today. By the way, Ruby and Jimmy may have left the South, but they sure didn't lose their Southern accents. I might have thought his was kind of a gimmick, but she's got the same one."

"I know. I think it's called the 'y'all chromosome'."

"I've never heard of anything like that. What are you talking about?" Marty asked.

"I read somewhere that people from the South have an added chromosome in their genetic makeup and that's why they talk like that," he said with a grin.

"Okay, Carl. For a moment you had me. Now back to work. You okay with my plan on how to divide up this appraisal?"

"Sounds fine with me. I had no idea Jimmy was as bad off as Ruby indicated. It's hard to believe after I saw his performance last night. Poor guy. It must be a real adjustment to be one of the top performers in the United States, travel all over the world, and then have everything, or almost everything taken away from you."

"Agreed. See you in a little while." Marty turned to Patron and said, "Patron, lie down. Here's your toy I brought so you'd feel comfortable." He obediently stretched out on the soft shag rug which was far warmer than the tile floor and promptly went to sleep with his pink flamingo plush toy firmly lodged between his paws.

CHAPTER NINE

Randy Allen sat at his desk in downtown Palm Springs thinking about the turn of events involving Jimmy Joseph. Jimmy had been his cash cow and client for more years than he could count.

When Jimmy was first starting out, Randy had spotted his talent, and offered to represent him for 15% of his gross earnings that came from entertaining, far less than what other agents were asking. Randy was just starting out as well, so he didn't have a very large bargaining chip. Randy had believed in Jimmy and was easily able to obtain bookings for him at major venues, first in the United States, and then in Europe.

Jimmy had made Randy rich beyond his wildest dreams, which was very fortunate for Randy, because his taste in women was costly. Randy came from the old school that if you wanted to sleep with a woman, you should marry her. And so he did. Five times. It was a good thing Randy's career had allowed him to have a very opulent lifestyle. Each of his wives had certainly enjoyed it, that is, until they decided it was time to divorce him.

After his second marriage had ended badly, with Randy making an out-of-court settlement rather than be saddled with alimony for the rest of his life, his therapist had some advice for him. That was something new, because Dr. Mertz never gave him advice, he simply asked Randy how he felt about something or let him vent over his imaginary and real problems. But this time was different. His therapist had told him in no uncertain terms that from now on he should just sleep with the women and not marry them.

Randy listened to the therapist and realized there probably was some truth to his words, but three months later he was in Las Vegas at the Graceland Wedding Chapel with wife number three. Jimmy had a long engagement at the Bellagio and Randy's latest wife was a backup singer for him. Six months later when she sued him for divorce, he rued not following his therapist's advice.

Las Vegas did Randy no favors. To his dismay, his next two marriages also ended in divorce and the only thing that kept him solvent was the amount of money Jimmy paid him. Without that, there was no doubt he'd be held in contempt of court for nonpayment of spousal support. The women he married were not stupid. They'd been around Vegas enough to know a rich mark when they saw one and unfortunately, Randy fit the description perfectly.

Now he was faced with the prospect of a serious drop in earnings. Serious enough that he wouldn't be able to pay his monthly spousal support payments. One of the other things his therapist had told him was that he should make absolutely certain that if he ever married again, he must have his wife-to-be sign a prenuptial agreement.

Randy had listened to his therapist and made an appointment with Jimmy's lawyer who said drawing up a prenuptial agreement was standard practice, particularly in Las Vegas, where marriages did not have a long shelf life.

Unfortunately, Randy had a romantic streak and thought asking his next wife-to-be to sign one would make him look like he took the marriage to be more of a business proposition than one of true love. Unfortunately, neither one of the last two wives fit that category, so now Randy was saddled with paying alimony to four wives. The fact that Jimmy's income had dropped by 90%, as had Randy's because of Jimmy's health condition, was causing Randy a lot of sleepless nights.

His accountant had called Randy and told him he needed to have his lawyer renegotiate the terms of his divorces, because there was no way he could meet his obligations and there was a good chance his ex-wives would sue him, and he'd be looking at wage garnishments and seizure of his bank accounts.

A few days earlier, in the middle of another sleepless night, he'd remembered that Jimmy told him once that Jimmy had made a large bequest in his trust to Randy. At the time Randy had thought Jimmy would outlive him by years, so he thanked Jimmy, but hadn't paid much attention to it. He sure could use that money now rather than later.

I wonder if there's any way Jimmy would advance me the money, he thought. *I'm going to ask him. After all, a lot of people with money choose to distribute some of it prior to their death.*

The next day he picked up the phone and called Jimmy. "Hey Jimmy, it's me. I've got a little problem, and I thought maybe you could help me out with it."

"Happy to, if I can," Jimmy said.

"Well, now that you're not earning what you used to, it means that my percentage is way down. In other words, I'm making about 10% of what I used to get paid by you. I've got a couple of obligations, like alimony for my ex-wives…"

Jimmy interrupted him. "Randy, me and everybody else told ya' not to marry them gold diggers. Any problems ya' got in that area, are yers' and yers' alone. Don't think I'll be helpin' ya' with 'em."

"Well, Jimmy, it's not exactly help that I need. I remember you told me once that you had made a large bequest in your trust to me. Sure could use it now," Randy said.

"I'm sure ya' could, but that ain't gonna' happen. Now that my health is pretty bad, don't know how much I'll even have left in my estate when I go. I'm even havin' an appraisal made of my memorabilia collection. If I go pretty soon, I'll probably donate it, but if not, might have to sell it to pay medical expenses. No, sorry, Randy, jes' ain't got them disposable funds like I used to. Tell them wives they rode the gravy train long enough. Gotta go, Ruby's here with my meds."

Randy stared with a blank look at the phone after Jimmy had hung up. He hadn't had a panic attack in a long time, but the way he felt now, he was pretty sure one was imminent. He felt boxed in with no way out.

Then he heard a little voice in his head, an insistent little voice.

"Randy, if Jimmy died now, you'd get the bequest because there is plenty of money now. Jimmy's health is failing, and he probably doesn't have long to live, anyway. Actually, you'd be doing him a favor by taking him out of his misery. As worn out as his body is, his immune system, couldn't fight anything. Wouldn't take much. Might do a little computer search on poison. There's a lot of them that might work for you. Think about it."

Later that morning, Randy did just that, and came up with the perfect plan. He'd get the money and no one would ever know it was him who caused the ultimate demise of Jimmy Joseph. He called the car rental agency at McCarran Airport and reserved a car for his trip to Palm Springs. This was going to be so easy he was sorry he hadn't thought of it before now.

CHAPTER TEN

Marty and Carl had been working all morning when the sound of a siren could be heard in the distance. A siren, particularly an ambulance siren, was unusual in a residential area such as Jimmy's. What was even more unusual was it kept getting louder and louder and then they heard loud voices as well. Patron had stood up, the guard hairs on his back erect, and he started to growl.

Carl walked into the room where Marty was and said, "What's going on? I'm hearing all kinds of voices, and I'd swear I heard a siren." He looked over at Patron and asked, "What's up with him?"

"I have no idea. I was just about to go in the house and ask Ruby what was going on. I'll put Patron's leash on him, so if someone is in there, he won't scare them."

"Well, I'm scared, if that's any consolation. I remember the last time Patron did that when we were on an appraisal and look what happened," he said. He was referring to when he and Marty were appraising a collection for a museum donation and Patron had gone ballistic when Carl had taken a knife down from a shelf and started writing down information about it.

"Okay, let's go," Marty said as she opened the door of the memorabilia house and walked by the pool towards the main house. The sound of voices became louder the closer they got to the house.

The main house was designed, as so many Palm Springs homes were, with a sweeping view through large glass walls from the front to the back.

"Oh no," Marty said. "Look, Carl, I can see an ambulance in the driveway. I hope nothing has happened to Jimmy."

They walked through the house to where the front door was standing wide open. Beyond it Mary could see Ruby gesturing and talking to the EMTs. A slightly built African American man, who Marty assumed was Ruby's brother, Horace, was standing next to Ruby. Marty and Carl hurried out the door to where they were standing.

"Ruby, what's happened?" Marty asked as Patron stood next to her, growling.

The EMT's backed the ambulance out of the driveway and quickly drove off, siren on. Ruby turned to her and said, "Dunno'. Jimmy was gone longer than usual to get the mail. Horace noticed it had been a long time and went out to the mailbox. When he got there, Jimmy was layin' there flat on his back in the driveway."

"Do you think he fell and knocked himself out?" Carl asked.

"Dunno'. Horace called 911 and then he called me. I ran out and we stayed with Jimmy 'til the ambulance got here. One of them EMTs said it looked like Jimmy'd been hit in the thigh by somethin'. Had no idea what it was."

"Do they think it was a gunshot?"

"I asked 'em, but they said they couldn't tell me nothin' and they'd know more after they got him to the hospital and a doctor saw him," Ruby said, as she fought to hold back tears.

"Ruby, you stay here. I'm goin' to the hospital. When Jimmy wakes up, he's gonna' want me there," Horace said, running towards the garage to get his car.

"Call me first thing, ya' hear?" Ruby hollered after him.

"I will. Jimmy's gonna' be jes' fine. He's gotta be," Horace shouted over his shoulder.

"Ruby, I think it would be better if Carl and I leave. You really don't need strangers in the house right now. I'll call you tomorrow, and we'll figure out a better time. Would that be alright with you?" Marty asked.

"Yes, I'd appreciate that. Even if you did have some questions for me, doubt if I could answer 'em, distracted as I am right now."

"I completely understand," Marty said, putting her hand on Ruby's shoulder. "Would you like me to lock up the memorabilia house for you?"

"Yes, thanks. My legs are a little shaky right now. Think I needs me to sit myself down for a spell. Horace might call me on the house phone, and I don't wanna' miss his call."

Carl and Marty walked back to the house where Jimmy's collection was stored and packed their appraising equipment. Marty was having a hard time with Patron. He hadn't stopped growling, and she was glad they were leaving. She wasn't looking forward to the ride back to Carl's antique shop with Carl and Patron.

As soon as they were in her car, Carl turned to her and said, "Any idea what's got Patron so spooked?"

"No, you know as much as I do. Do you think Jimmy fell or do you think it was something more?"

"I have no idea, Marty, you're the amateur sleuth, not me. I will tell you that based on Patron alone, I'll bet something more than feeling faint and falling down happened to Jimmy. Mark my words, this is going to be another one of your murder appraisals."

"Well, I certainly hope not. I really like Jimmy, and it looks like

Ruby and Horace are totally devoted to him. I'd hate it if something happened to him."

Carl grumbled something in a low tone.

"I'm sorry, Carl, I didn't catch what you said."

"I said maybe you should name your business 'Murder Appraisals.'

"Carl, that's a low blow. You know as well as I do that I've never done anything to cause murders to happen when I'm appraising. Today you were near me all morning, and nothing I did could even remotely be attached to a murder. And speaking of murder, we certainly don't know if Jimmy was murdered. In fact, we don't know if he's dead. He was alive when they took him to the hospital. And if something does happen to him, it probably wouldn't be all that unusual given the condition of his health."

"All of that is true, but have you ever wondered why a number of your appraisals have included murder? I mean, Marty, it's not normal. I like you, and I like working with you, but if we find out Jimmy was murdered, I may have to take a pass on any more appraisals with you. My heart can't take it anymore."

"Carl, we're a great team and maybe these things happen to me because I've been very lucky in helping solve some murders. Maybe the universe thinks that if someone is going to be murdered, I should be the one doing the appraisal because I can solve them."

"That's about the most convoluted explanation of anything I've ever heard."

"Carl, speak English. What does convoluted mean?"

"It means extremely complex and difficult to follow, and that's what you always do when the subject of you, murder, and your appraisals comes up." When Marty pulled up in front of Carl's antique shop he said, "Look, I'm sure you'll find out something from Jeff about Jimmy. I'd appreciate you letting me know. Sure wish I'd gotten the money from him for the Elvis jacket before he went out to the mailbox."

Mailbox. That's what Laura was talking about? I know Jimmy is going to die and that means someone murdered him. The doctors may not know yet, but I do, she thought.

"Of course, Carl. I'll let you know the minute I hear anything. Let's keep our fingers crossed that he just fell down and he'll be home tomorrow."

"Yeah," Carl said as he got out of her car, "Just keep talking the happy talk, but we both know how it's gonna' shake out."

He walked around to the trunk of her car which she'd popped open and retrieved his appraisal equipment. "Here's what I did this morning," he said handing her his notes and a cartridge from his handheld dictation device. "Figure you'll want to get started on this and who knows when we'll be going back. I'll email you the photos I took."

"Thanks Carl. I'll get this to Edy, so she can start working on the rough draft for Ruby to take a look at. I'll do a little research on what both of us did this afternoon, too."

"Yeah, like I said, let me know if you hear anything." Without a backward glance, Carl turned and walked into his antique shop.

"Patron, I have a feeling he's right and you know he's right, don't you?"

Patron didn't respond one way or the other to Marty's inquiry. He'd become very calm as soon as they'd left Jimmy's home, and he simply stayed quiet and wagged his tail after they left Carl's shop. When they arrived at the desert compound, he was a far different dog than he'd been only a short while earlier.

CHAPTER ELEVEN

When Marty and Patron walked into the courtyard of the compound, they were immediately greeted by Duke, her big black Labrador retriever, with what Marty assumed to be a quizzical expression on his face. It was as if he was asking, "How come you took Patron and not me?"

Marty decided the answer would be too complicated to explain to him and instead, went to her house, made lunch, and spent the afternoon researching what she and Carl had seen that morning during the abbreviated appraisal at Jimmy Joseph's home. That afternoon, she sent the photos they'd taken to Lucy at the Hi-Lo Drugstore, so she could have the photos she needed to accompany the rough draft.

At 5:30 she saved what she'd been working on, stood up from her computer, and went to the kitchen to feed Duke and Patron. She heard voices coming from the courtyard and figured some of the compound members were sharing the events of the day over a glass of wine. It was a habit they'd gotten into before enjoying one of John's dinners, and tonight was no exception.

When she walked into the courtyard, the little twinkling lights on the trees had been turned on, and since it was early spring and there was a chill in the air, someone had already turned on the three tall patio heaters. As always, it was a magical place, what with the over-the-top landscaping and of course, the peaceful quiet of the desert as night time approached. Laura had a green thumb, and she was the one responsible for the abundance of blooming flowers and ferns that ringed the large courtyard and were also hanging from the trees.

Marty walked over to the table where Laura and Les were sitting. "Evening, everyone. How was your day?" she asked as she poured herself a glass of wine.

"Probably better than yours," Laura said.

"What are you talking about? Carl and I spent the morning at Jimmy Josephs' home doing an appraisal of his memorabilia collection. "Unfortunately, he took a fall and had to be rushed to the hospital."

"Then I guess you haven't heard the news. It's on every channel on television."

"Laura, I have no idea what you're talking about. Please, fill me in."

"Jimmy Joseph died this afternoon. He never regained consciousness. He developed a terribly high fever after he was admitted to the hospital, and then he died. One newscaster said there was talk of murder, because the coroner found a small round pellet-like object in his leg which also showed an entry wound."

Marty stared at her, mouth agape. When she was finally able to speak, she said, "I can't believe it. If he was murdered, that means we were there when it happened. Oh my gosh. He really was a nice man. I wonder who did it? Did the news reports say anything about that?"

Just then the gate to the courtyard opened and Jeff walked in, greeted excitedly by Duke and Patron. "I can answer that. The answer is no, at this time we have nothing to go on. His home has been yellow-taped. I was over there late this afternoon and his housekeeper and right-hand man were too distraught to talk, so I told them I'd take their statements in the morning."

He turned to Marty and said, "You were there this morning. Did you see anything suspicious or that would lead you to think that something bad might happen?"

Marty looked at Laura. "The only thing I know is what I told you on the phone this morning, that Laura was concerned and so was Patron. I don't know if I told you that Laura had a vision of a mailbox. Jimmy was getting his mail when whatever happened, happened. That's about all I know."

"Did you have the sense that Jimmy was concerned about anything? Did he act nervous? Did he say or do anything that would lead you to believe he'd been threatened?"

"Not a thing, Jeff. We didn't actually spend too much time with him. He met us at the door and then took us to where his collection was stored. His personal assistant, Ruby, made him go back to the main house and rest while she walked us through the rooms of the building where his collection is housed."

"Laura, your turn. You were the one who got the vibes before anything happened. What are you getting now?"

She sat quietly for several moments with her eyes closed while Marty, Les, and Jeff closely watched her. Eventually she opened her eyes and said, "I'm seeing revenge, greed, and a great deal of anger. I'm sorry but that's all I'm getting. Just emotions, but no people."

Laura turned to Marty and said, "I'm getting a very, very strong sense that you will become involved in solving this murder, and that's what it is. The coroner will be confirming it shortly. She turned to Jeff, "You won't be able to work much on this murder because unfortunately, there are too many other murders happening in Palm Springs right now, and you'll be needed in a number of other places."

"Great, that was not what I wanted to hear. Guess I just wait for the other shoe to drop. I'm starved. Are we on our own tonight or did John leave something for us?" Jeff said as he looked around.

"He and Max had a catering job tonight, but he told me this morning that he'd left a beef stew casserole for us along with some soda bread. I put the casserole in the oven several hours ago and it's ready whenever all of you are," Laura said.

"I'd like to eat now if the rest of you don't mind. I expect tonight to be a long one. That darned art muse of mine won't let go and is harassing me to finish a painting. I fear it may be another long night," Les said.

"Yeah, and if Laura's premonitions are right, it may be for me too. Let's eat," Jeff added.

"You all sit. I was here all afternoon, and I'm pretty rested. I'll bring it out," Marty said.

A few moments later she walked out of John's house with a large pot of stew. Laura had gotten up to help her and they brought out the individual avocado and orange salads as well as the soda bread John had mentioned.

It was quiet as they ate, each one thinking about Jimmy's murder and what others might be occurring locally. Laura was the first to speak. "I don't know how John does it, but night after night it's just one fabulous meal after another. This is probably the best stew I've ever had and he could easily make it ahead of time and serve it at the Red Pony food trucks."

"Agreed," Marty said, "and I really like the salad. It's light and plays beautifully with the heaviness of the stew. Plus, I saw some scrumptious looking cookies on the counter. I'll go get them."

She walked back to John's house and then returned with a plate of cookies and a piece of paper. "He left a note under the cookies. He calls them double chocolate espresso walnut cookies. They look delicious," she said as she set them down in the center of the table.

"They not only look delicious, they are delicious. Actually, these might be the best chocolate cookies I've ever had, and I can taste a hint of coffee in them," Les said as he took two more of the cookies.

"I'll leave a note for John and tell him what a hit dinner was," Marty said as Jeff's phone rang.

"It's starting, Jeff," Laura said. "Better clear your calendar for the next few days."

Jeff looked over at her, took his phone out of his pocket, and left the courtyard. He returned a few minutes later and said, "Marty, Laura was right. I've got to leave, and I doubt that I'll be home for the rest of the night. Three people were killed at the concert. Seems like they were able to sneak guns into the concert as well as some illegal drugs. Nasty combination.

"Hate to ask this of you Marty, but since you were with the two people who work and live at Jimmy's house today, would you mind going there tomorrow and talking to them? I'll take formal statements in a day or so, but I don't want the case to get cold just because I have to spend time on the latest murders."

"Of course, Jeff. What time were you going to meet them?"

"I told them I'd be there at 10:00. You could reschedule if that doesn't work for you."

"No, that's fine. I'd already cleared my schedule to do Jimmy's appraisal. I'll probably stop by the Hi-Lo and see if the photos I sent Lucy earlier in the day are ready. Happy to help."

"See you later, probably much later," Jeff said as he kissed her cheek and then gave each of the dogs a pat on the head. A moment later they heard his car pulling out of the driveway.

"Les, take off," Laura said. "I can tell you're anxious to get back to the muse. Marty and I will finish up here."

Half an hour later, dishes done, and dogs walked, Marty got in bed, wondering what tomorrow would bring.

CHAPTER TWELVE

Marty's cell phone rang at 7:00 the next morning. She looked at the screen and saw it was Jeff.

"Hi, honey. How bad was it last night?" she asked.

"About as bad as it gets. In addition to the three people who were killed, several bystanders were also injured. I have to spend most of the day out at the concert area, doing everything I can to speed up the investigation process. The performers were paid a lot of money, and we can't allow them to go on stage until my men finish with the crime scene. In other words, no one can perform, and the public is barred from admission. Everyone, from the food truck people to the promoter, are taking a big financial hit."

"Any word on the cause of Jimmy's death?"

"I saw the coroner briefly about an hour ago, and he told me to treat it as a homicide. He found ricin in the pellet he removed from Jimmy's thigh."

"Wasn't that the substance somebody put into envelopes and sent to a bunch of legislators a few years ago? As I remember, it was a real hot news topic for a while. I kind of remember they got the guy who sent the letters. Sound right?"

"Good memory. He was from Utah, and yes, law enforcement authorities did catch him. The problem with this poison is that it's so easy for anyone to get. It's produced from the castor bean plant, and that is not a rare plant. It's a constant headache for medical and law enforcement personnel."

"Have you told Ruby and Horace that Jimmy was murdered?"

"No, I haven't had a chance to do anything. I only had it confirmed about it an hour ago. I felt 6:00 a.m. is too early for me to be calling people who have just had an emotional shock. Hate to ask this, Marty, but that's the reason I'm calling. The coroner told me he's not releasing his results to the news media or anybody else until he does his final report which will be tomorrow or the next day. I don't think Jimmy's staff will have any way of knowing it's been confirmed that it was murder unless you tell them. My men will be at the house today doing crime investigative work, but even they don't know.

"Anyway, I'd appreciate it if you would tell them. I don't want them to hear about it tomorrow on the news or from someone calling them. At least you've established a relationship with them, and you're good at stuff like this. Again, sorry to ask you to do it. I would, but my hands are full at the moment. I'll pay you back."

"Yes, you will. I'm thinking Europe, Hawaii, maybe even Hong Kong. I've never been there. What do you think?"

"Would you settle for a movie and a good dinner?" Jeff asked.

"Can't top John's dinners, so I'll settle for a movie and Jeff, you know I'm really letting you off the hook with this one."

"I know, Marty. Call me after you talk to them and tell me how it went. I've got another call I have to take. Love you," he said as he ended the call.

*****

"Well, well, well, if it ain't my favorite garage sale lady," Lucy, the manager of the photo department at the Hi-Lo Drugstore said when Marty walked into the store. "Jes' kiddin' Marty. Know the stuff ya' look at ain't never gonna' see a garage. And man, those pics you sent me yesterday are somethin' else. Woo Hoo! Bet that stuff is worth a purty penny."

"And hello to you, Lucy. Yes, those things I appraised yesterday will come in at a purty penny as you call it. From that, I assume the photos are ready for me."

"Sure 'nuf. Here they are. By the way, where's that little bundle of white knowin' dog?"

"White knowin' dog? I'm afraid I don't understand what you mean."

"Talkin' about the little bundle of cuteness ya' got recently. Ya' know. The one with that SP thing."

"Lucy, I think you mean ESP, and I left that little bundle of cuteness in the car."

"Well, that's too bad. He probably coulda' tol' us who offed Jimmy Joseph."

"What do you mean?"

"Aw, c'mon, Marty. Everybody knows a big star like Jimmy Joseph gots lotsa' enemies. Walkin' out to get his mail and he jes' happens to fall down. Right. Bet all the stock I got in cannabis that guy got whacked by one of 'em."

"Wait a minute, Lucy. You're going a little too fast here for me. I assume you found out that Jimmy Joseph died, but I don't believe anything has been said that would indicate he was murdered."

"May not be sayin' it, but I know it, ya' know it, and I bet your furry friend knows it, too."

"Lucy, somehow I don't see you investing in cannabis stock. I mean I know it's legal in California now, but you've told me before how opposed you are to drugs. This doesn't sound like you."

"Yeah, that was the old Lucy, before I got religion."

"You got religion? How?"

"Well, ya' know me and the ol' man have a dog, Killer. Well, Killer started whimperin' every time we touched his leg. We took him in to see the vet and he tol' us that Killer had dislocated his hip. He set it and said instead of givin' Killer some drugs, he tol' us to go to the cannabis store in Palm Springs and get, I think he called it, a topical cream. Said it would help Killer with his pain."

"Lucy, are you telling me that you and your husband went to a cannabis store in Palm Springs?"

"Yep, and man was it somethin'. Totally different than what I expected. Coulda' eaten off the floor, it was so clean. Had three armed guards and no weirdos in sight. Mattera' fact, most of the people in there was older than me and my ol' man. Heard they was buyin' that stuff for what they call 'dicinal purposes.' Always thought that was a bunch of bull, but if'n ya' coulda' seen the change in Killer, it'd make a believer outta ya'."

"The word is medicinal purposes, Lucy. So let me get this straight. You went to the cannabis store, bought something for Killer, and he's much better. And now you're buying cannabis stock?"

"Yep. Figure cannabis is where alcohol was after Prohibition. Wanna' get on that gravy train 'fore it leaves the station, ya' know? We got all them lennials comin' up that probably smoked the stuff and now they're gettin' old and gots all kinds of aches and pains, and ya' can plan on them buyin' the dicinal stuff. Figure I'm gonna' get rich purty quick."

"This is definitely not a conversation that I ever expected to have with you, but I'll be curious how Killer does and how your stock does. I'm sorry to cut this conversation short, but I have an appointment and need to leave."

"Not quite yet, girl. Ya' know how every mornin' I get me a quote for my day. Well, today's jes' beats all. Ol' man is always gettin' testy with me 'cuz I run a little late. Anyway, listen to this," Lucy said as she pulled a piece of paper out of her pocket.

"Jes' closed my eyes this mornin' and let my finger pick a page. Here's what it opened to. This here is a quote from Confucius. Guess he was some famous Chinese guy from a long time ago. Says 'It does not matter how slowly you go as long as you do not stop.' Don't that jes' beat all? Can't wait to show it to my ol' man. I mean if it was good enuf' for Confucius, oughtta' be good enuf' for the ol' man."

Marty just looked at Lucy, wondering if she was in some parallel universe and if this conversation had really happened. She was trying to think of something appropriate to say when Lucy handed her a dog cookie and said, "Tell that white knowin' dog this is a present from his friend Lucy."

"Thanks, Lucy, I will. And thanks for the quick service. I really appreciate it."

"No problem. Yer' on my VIP list. Tell that handsome hubby of yers' hi fer me."

"Will do," Marty said as she walked out the door. She got in her car and gave the dog cookie to Patron. "Here, you knowin' dog, a treat from Lucy." She could swear that Patron was smiling at her.

CHAPTER THIRTEEN

The gates were open at the Joseph estate and Marty could see several law enforcement cars as she drove toward the house, parking her car in the circular driveway. She hadn't wanted to bring Patron, based on his performance yesterday, but given that a murder had taken place at the estate, she thought Patron needed to be with her. Truth be told, she felt a lot safer with the big dog next to her.

They walked up to the door and rang the bell. A moment later it was opened by Ruby, her pain clearly etched on her face. "Come on in, Marty. Yer' husband called and told me what happened out at the music festival and that you'd be takin' his place."

"Thank you. I hope you don't mind, but I brought Patron along with me as well. Given everything that's happened, my husband felt it would be for the best. Is Horace here?"

"Yes, he's waitin' for us in the livin' room," she said as they walked down the hall. "He's havin' a real hard time with this."

"I can only imagine what you two are going through," Marty said as they walked into the living room. She sat down in a chair, smiled at Horace, and said, "I'm sorry I'm not back here under entirely different circumstances."

She looked at both of them and said, "I have something I need to tell you. Since Jeff couldn't come today, he asked me to tell you in his absence. He felt that it should be done in person. He found out early this morning from the coroner that Jimmy was murdered. The coroner found a poison called ricin in a pellet he removed from Jimmy's leg."

They were both quiet for several moments, digesting what Marty had just told them. Tears began to slide down Ruby's cheeks, and she made no attempt to wipe them away.

After several moments Horace said, "Don't understand how that could be. Everybody loved Jimmy. That man didn't have a mean bone in his body. I've seen him help all kinds of people. Whoever did it was some kind of a monster. Jimmy didn't deserve this." His eyes filled with tears and he took a red bandanna out of his pocket, and tried, with little success, to wipe them away.

Marty looked away from Horace to give him time to compose himself. She glanced down at Patron who was sitting at her feet and had been looking at Horace when he spoke. His guard hairs were raised along his back.

What's up with that? Marty thought. *He's not growling, but he's clearly not a friend of Horace's. I'll have to ask Laura about it when I get back to the compound.*

"I agree," Marty said, "but it looks like there was someone who didn't share your opinion of Jimmy. What I would like both of you to do is start thinking of any problems Jimmy might have had with people in the last few weeks or months, no matter how minor they might seem to you. My husband would like me to make a list of possible suspects, or people who might be considered persons of interest, right away. In a case like this, time is of the essence."

She waited a few moments and then continued, "Can either of you think of anything Jimmy said about having words with someone or a negative feeling about someone? Just reach back in your mind and think for a few minutes."

Ruby was the first to speak. "His sister called Jimmy 'bout a week ago. Jimmy thought she'd married a real loser years ago and pretty much wrote her off. He tol' me once that he didn't regret doin' it, but he'd left a little something for her in his trust. He called it guilt money."

"Yes, go on," Marty said, as Ruby began to tear up again.

"Well, he was purty mad after he got off the phone. Tol' me the only reason she'd called was to get some money fer her no-good son, leastways that's how Jimmy referred to him. Didn't hear any more about it, but she's family, so I'd think that would take her offa' any suspect list."

"Not necessarily," Marty said. "Stranger things have happened."

"I can think of a couple of people now that ya' mention it," Horace said. "First of all, his agent, Randy Allen, called Jimmy and asked him if he'd give him the money that Jimmy was gonna' leave him in his trust, now, rather than when he died. Tol' Jimmy he needed it to pay his alimony."

"Why now?" Marty asked.

"Well, Jimmy was makin' a lotta' money when he was performin' in Vegas, and Randy was gettin' fifteen percent of everthin'. Had been fer all these years. Then Jimmy had the heart attack and couldn't work in Vegas no more. Heard Jimmy say he was only makin' one-tenth of what he used to make, which would mean Randy was down 90%. That man jes' had a thing for marryin' women.

"Everybody, including Jimmy, tol' him to jes' sleep with 'em, but that boy had some itch that he needed to marry 'em. Problem was, they was all gold diggers and left him after a while. Guy ended up payin' alimony to a bunch of 'em."

"Okay, that's two possible suspects. Who else can you think of?" she said to both of them.

Ruby spoke up. "That new neighbor next door. Leastways she's somewhat new. Bought the property 'bout a year ago. Jimmy told me she met him at the mailbox one day and they had words about them Mexican Fan Palm trees in Jimmy's back yard. She said they were an eyesore. Jimmy planted them himself, so he didn't take kindly to her sayin' that. Guess they kind of left each other on not very good terms."

"Seems kind of like an insignificant thing to kill someone over, but you'd be surprised at some of the things that motivate a person to commit murder. Do you know her name or anything about her?" Marty asked.

"Yeah. Her name is Carla McIntyre. I remember readin' in The Desert Sun that she'd bought the house next to Jimmy Joseph's. She'd been an actress several years ago, but retired, sayin' that all the roles now were for younger women and she was gonna' enjoy life in the desert and not have to try scroungin' for roles she never got. Sounded kind of bitter, if ya' ask me."

"I'll talk to her when I leave. Which side does she live on?"

"She's lives on the left side as yer' lookin' at Jimmy's house. He said she was a looker, but had a real nasty side," Horace interjected.

"I don't know about you, Marty, but I sure could use some coffee 'bout now. Mind if we take a break while I make some?" Ruby asked.

"Not at all. I agree. I think we could use a break about now. Let's have some coffee and resume when we're finished. I think if Jeff were here, he'd do the same."

CHAPTER FOURTEEN

"Thanks, Ruby. That coffee really helped. Okay, let's get back to the suspect list. Can either of you think of anyone else that should be on it?" Marty asked.

"Horace," Ruby said, "whatta' 'bout that guy that used to perform at the Red Velvet Lounge? I 'member Jimmy saying somethin' about the owner tellin' him that the guy wasn't too happy when Jimmy replaced him. I guess he tried to convince the owner that he and Jimmy should both play there, but the owner wouldn't go fer it. Am I right?"

"Yeah, but that's about all I can remember too. I don't think Jimmy ever even talked to the guy. As soon as the Velvet owner heard that the doctor weren't gonna' let Jimmy travel no more, he offered Jimmy the gig at the Velvet. Weren't nothin' like where Jimmy performed in Vegas, but I remember he said it would keep him from bein' bored."

"It's probably nothing, Horace, but if you can come up with the guy's name, I'd like to have it."

Horace was quiet, obviously trying to recall the man's name. "Ain't 100% on this, but seems like I used to see an ad in The Desert Sun for a guy named Miles Reed. The ad always had him sittin' at a piano and it kind of reminded me of Jimmy when he was playin' in

Vegas. That's why I remember it."

Marty wrote it down. "I agree, it's probably nothing, but since there's not all that much to go on, it's worth checking into. Anything else?"

"Man, I don't know where this came from, but I remember a coupla' weeks ago I was sittin' in Jimmy's backstage room at the Velvet when the manager came in and told Jimmy about a fan who wanted to talk to him after his performance. Had her business card in his hand. Reason I remember it is he told Jimmy he'd pass if it was him, 'cuz the woman was the ugliest human being he'd ever seen."

"Wow, that's harsh. Did the woman overhear that?"

"I have no idea."

"Do you think the manager would remember her name?"

"Again, ain't got no idea, but I think I might still have her business card," Horace said.

"Why would you have saved it?"

"Jimmy had a computer file that I kept with the names and addresses of his fans. Coupla' times a year he'd send out a newsletter to them, tellin' them where he was scheduled to play, and things like that. After his heart attack, we sent one out tellin' his fans he was fine, but his doctor preferred that he didn't travel. He said somethin' about if they was ever in the Palm Springs area, to go see him at the Red Velvet Lounge. Guess old habits die hard. I jes' always took business cards and saved them. Let me go to my office and see if I can find it."

Patron watched him go, again, the hackles on his back standing on end, but he was quiet. Marty had never seen him behave quite like this. He was either a complete "lap dog" or doing a 180, barking and growling at some perceived menace. The only thing she could think of was that it had something to do with yesterday and the discovery that Jimmy had been injured.

Horace returned a few minutes later and said, "Here it is. Thought I had it. Ugly one's name is Priscilla Simpson. Also has her telephone number and an address on it. Looks like a residence to me," he said, handing the card to Marty.

"Thanks. I'm sure this is a complete longshot, but I know Jeff would want everyone's name, no matter how far down the list of possible suspects they might be. I'll add hers to it and see what happens."

"Marty, if we're finished, I need to think about sendin' a newsletter to Jimmy's fans. With everything that's happened in the last twenty-four hours, it never occurred to me. But now that the subject of his fan file has been brought up, it's only right that I send somethin' out about his death."

"I agree, and I can't thank you enough for meeting with me. Again, my thoughts are with both of you. It's hard enough when someone we care for greatly dies, but I'm sure it's vastly harder to discover they've been murdered, but please don't put that in the newsletter.

"Trust me, my husband and his department will do everything they can to find the person who killed Jimmy. If either of you think of anything else, please call me. You have my number. I'll be back in a few days to finish up the appraisal. Again, thanks for your time."

Marty stood up and motioned for Patron to follow her. Patron looked over his shoulder at Horace and Ruby, but willingly followed her.

CHAPTER FIFTEEN

When Marty was back in her car, she looked at the dashboard clock and realized that she'd spent over two hours at the Joseph home talking to Ruby and Horace. She was starving and decided to get some lunch at an In N' Out hamburger fast food drive thru.

Minutes later she gave her order to the young clerk at the drive-thru window, "I'd like a double cheese, animal style, animal fries, and an iced tea. Oh, and two plain hamburger patties. Thanks." Marty was not a fan of fast food places, but this particular one was practically an institution in California. She knew of no other hamburger place that served their burgers and fries "animal style" meaning extra Thousand Island dressing, mustard on the patties, and extra pickles on the burger with the fries being topped with cheese and grilled onions.

The one time she'd given Patron an animal style burger, he'd turned his nose up at it, clearly not a fan of dressing, but she knew she wasn't the only one who had made In N' Out their favorite fast-food place. She remembered reading a newspaper article about some fraternity members at the University of California, Santa Barbara, who had their pledges drive to the nearest In N' Out and bring back sacks of hamburgers. At the time the nearest one was in Carpinteria, requiring almost an hour round trip.

She'd noticed a dog park on her way to the Joseph house and

decided that she and Patron could eat in the car and then she'd give him some exercise and socialization time at the park.

Patron had definitely liked his plain hamburger patties and when he was finished, he was ready to run it off. Marty unlatched, entered, and then closed the two gates that led into the dog park. Patron was immediately in heaven sniffing the other dogs who had come to greet him. While he ran and played with his new friends, Marty sat on a bench and began texting Jeff with the suspect list she'd gotten from Ruby and Horace that morning.

She looked at her watch and saw that she'd spent almost an hour composing the text to him, which was quite long. She sent it and sat back, watching Patron as he raced back and forth across the dog park area. He was easily one of the larger dogs, but even so, the fact that so many little dogs were running with him indicated that they felt safe with him.

I just wish I understood his behavior earlier today, Marty thought. *I really don't know what to make of it. He was clearly in protection mode, but did none of the other things he's done before. Maybe he's just maturing and the barking and growling are gone. I need to talk to Laura tonight and get her thoughts.*

Her cell phone pinged indicating she had a message which she assumed was from Jeff. It was, and he thanked her for finding out as much as she had and that he'd see her at dinner that evening.

She called out to Patron, who unwillingly trotted over to her. She snapped on his leash and said, "Sorry, big guy, but I need to go see one of the possible suspects. You can nap in the car. Say goodbye to all your new four-legged friends."

Marty had been certain for a long time that Patron understood everything she said and today was no exception. He turned back towards his admiring fans and yipped as if to say, "It's been fun. See you next time."

*****

The dog park was just a short distance from Jimmy's home and his next-door neighbor. When Marty drove by, she noticed the entry gate to Carla McIntyre's home was open, so she turned in and drove up the driveway. The house and yard were kept private by a thick hedge on both sides of the property, effectively shutting the house and front yard off to a neighbor's view.

Marty turned off the engine and opened the car windows so Patron could get some fresh air while she was gone. However, the more she thought about it, she realized that meeting with someone who could possibly be a murderer without Patron beside her would not please Jeff. Plus, it could be deadly for her.

She didn't want to frighten the woman by taking the big dog with her, so she rolled the windows down further, making a compromise with herself and her mixed emotions. If Patron was as psychically inclined as Laura said he was, he'd know if Marty needed his protection and he could get out of the car through one of the windows. She also knew he was well-enough trained that he wouldn't frivolously jump out the window, plus he was tired from the dog park and the two hamburger patties he'd eaten earlier.

Marty walked up to the bright red doors and rang the doorbell. A moment later someone came to the door and a voice came through the intercom, "How can I help you?"

"My name is Marty Malone, and I'd like to speak to Carla McIntyre. It's regarding her neighbor, Jimmy Joseph."

The door was opened by a very attractive blond woman who looked to be in her forties. She wore a coral silk short-sleeved blouse and white silk slacks, which contrasted beautifully with her deep tan. Gold earrings and a necklace further set off her tan. On her right hand was a huge marquise cut diamond surrounded by smaller marquise diamonds. The effect was of a large flower surrounded by petals.

"I'm Carla McIntyre. What can I help you with?"

"May I come in? I'll only be a few minutes."

The woman thought for a few moments and then said, "Yes, we can talk in my study, but it will have to be short, since my agent will be here momentarily." She closed the door behind her and indicated for Marty to follow her down the hall. They entered a study with bookcases lining the walls.

Carla motioned for Marty to sit on a couch that faced the unlit fireplace and said, "Now, what is this all about?"

Marty took a deep breath and said, "I'm a friend of Jimmy Joseph's. You may have noticed the ambulance at Mr. Joseph's yesterday, as well as the law enforcement cars that are there today."

"No, I was gone yesterday and I haven't been out of the house today. Why, did Mr. Joseph suffer another heart attack, although I doubt that would necessitate the law enforcement cars. Is he having some kind of a problem?"

"Unfortunately, Mr. Joseph died last night. The coroner has confirmed it was murder."

Carla's eyes became wide and she said, "Oh no. What happened? Are you with the police?"

"No, my husband is the head detective in the case. He's swamped with some other cases, and asked me if I could do a little legwork. Anyway, we don't know exactly what happened. As a neighbor, I thought maybe you might have heard or seen something that could be helpful in determining who the killer was. At least that's the reason I came here, but seeing how private your home is from your neighbor's, you probably didn't."

"No, I only talked to him once and that was about a week ago. I introduced myself to him and then we talked for a few minutes. The conversation turned to the Mexican Fan Palms he has in his back yard and how I think they're the ugliest things I've ever seen. They're the first thing anyone talks about when they go into my back yard. Nothing is said about the infinity pool I had installed. All anyone talks about are those stupid palm trees."

"You mentioned you were gone yesterday. Can anyone corroborate that?" Marty asked.

"If you're thinking that I could be a suspect, better think again. I was reading for a role in a movie, and as a matter of fact I got it. That's why my agent is on his way here now. In answer to your question, yes, probably twenty people can vouch for my whereabouts.

"I don't know what time Mr. Joseph was murdered, but I didn't get back from Los Angeles until around 10:00 last night after leaving the house at 7:00 yesterday morning. I met my agent in Los Angeles at 9:00 a.m. When was he murdered?"

"He was murdered around 11:15 yesterday morning."

"Well, in that case I have a solid alibi with a lot of witnesses. I was literally reading for the role at that time. I stayed in Los Angeles and met friends for dinner. I figured a celebration was in order."

"I won't take up any more of your time, Ms. McIntyre," Marty said as she stood up, "and congratulations on getting the role. Will you be staying here or moving to Los Angeles?"

"I'll be staying here. The movie is going to be shot on location in Hawaii. Maybe my tan had something to do with me getting the role. In any event, I'll see what happens from here. I just hope whoever is going to take over Mr. Joseph's house cuts down those horrible eyesores."

She walked Marty to the front door and said, "Please, talk to the people who are going to live in the house and tell them the neighbors are up in arms about those awful palm trees."

"I'll see what I can do," Marty said as she left and walked to her car. She got in, looked at Patron, who opened one eye as if to say "I knew you didn't need me, so I slept."

What a cold person, Marty thought on her drive home. *She was far more concerned about the Mexican Fan Palm trees than she was about the fact that her next-door neighbor had been murdered. I hope her return to the world of entertainment is short-lived.*

CHAPTER SIXTEEN

A half hour later Marty pulled into the driveway of the compound. No cars were in the driveway and Les kept his in the garage, because he rarely left the compound, spending most of his time painting his highly sought-after art works.

Marty's black Labrador retriever, Duke, was waiting by the gate for her and Patron to return, his usual place when Marty was gone. He slept there until she returned.

"Duke, we're back. Looks like it's just you, me, and Patron, although Les is probably in his studio. Come on, let's take a minute to enjoy the desert, and then we'll go in and you can go back to sleep while I work."

The dogs took some time looking for little critters moving around on the desert floor and were rewarded by seeing several lizards. They soon got bored, took care of their business, and Marty brought them into her house so they could sleep. She changed her clothes, booted up her computer, and spent the next three hours reviewing auction results for memorabilia objects.

"Okay, guys. I'm sufficiently brain dead," she said to the two dogs. "Time to meet the group in the courtyard and see what special treat John has in store for dinner for us tonight. Ready to join me? Oh, and did I mention that it's probably time for dinner for both of you?"

At the word "dinner" both of the dogs stood up from their beds and trotted into the kitchen. It was pretty much a nightly occurrence – they got their dinner before Marty joined the others, and tonight was no exception.

After she finished feeding the dogs, she walked into the courtyard where Laura and Les were sitting, sharing the day's events. Sometimes Les came to the table with paint smudges on both himself and his clothes, but tonight he was spot free, and from the dampness of his hair, Marty assumed two things. One, that he'd just stepped out of his shower, and two, because he was free from paint smudges, he'd finished whatever painting he'd been working on.

"Hi, guys. How is my favorite sister and my favorite artist?"

"Your favorite sister is great and wants to hear what happened at the Joseph house today," Laura said as she poured Marty a glass of wine.

"And your favorite painter just finished what I consider my best one yet. I'm kind of sorry it's already promised to someone, because I'd like to see what it would bring in a gallery. And I'm also just as interested as Laura in finding out what happened to you today."

"I'll fill you in when everyone is here, then I won't have to repeat myself. Jeff texted me that he'll be home for dinner. Where's John?"

"He was here, but he said he wanted to take care of a few things before dinner. Max is with him. Evidently we're having a skillet cooked cod fish with a lemon caper sauce tonight."

"Yum, that sounds great. I haven't had cod all that much. I never saw it on a menu when I lived in the Midwest," Marty said.

"Haven't seen it around here all that much either, but I'm looking forward to it. Always liked it when I had it," Les said.

They heard a car pull into the driveway and immediately Patron and Duke hurried over to the gate.

"Between the sound of the car and the actions of Patron and Duke, I think we can safely assume that your husband will be here imminently," Les said.

A moment later Jeff walked in with a large briefcase. He stopped just inside the courtyard to greet Duke and Patron, who were beside themselves with joy.

"Be there in a minute, guys. I want to change clothes and get rid of this gun. I think you'll all feel better sitting there with me if it isn't in sight. I've noticed it has a dampening effect on social situations."

Just then John and Max walked into the courtyard with a platter containing different kinds of cheese, salami, and crackers, along with some small serving plates. "I wanted to hear what Jeff had to say about everything as well as your day, Marty, so I thought we could have some appetizers before I start the cod. It's one of those things that cooks fast and needs to be watched. *Mangia, mangia*," he said as he set the platter down on the big table.

"Thanks, John. I just realized I never had time for lunch, so stop me if I monopolize the appetizers. I'll try to leave a few for all of you," Jeff said, loading up one of the small plates with items from the platter. With his mouth full, he said, "Marty, why don't you tell everyone what you found out? Pretty much the things you texted to me, and then I'll tell them what I found out."

Marty spent the next half hour recounting her meeting with Ruby and Horace regarding the identity of possible suspects. Then she told them about her conversation with Carla McIntyre. She ended by saying, "Jeff, before you begin, I'd like to get Laura's opinion on something that happened with Patron while I was with Horace and Ruby."

"Have at it. I'm happy just chowing down on this stuff. By the way, John, the cheese samples are really unique."

"Thanks. A new cheese shop just opened in La Quinta. They've got a lot of Wisconsin types of cheese. Think they're appealing to the snowbirders who come to the Palm Springs area from the northern part of the country and Canada."

"My turn," Marty said. "While I was at the Joseph home today, I was talking to Horace and Ruby and Patron was lying by my feet. Whenever Horace would talk, the hackles on Patron's back would stand up. He was alert, looking at Horace, but he never once barked or growled. Considering that Horace is the last person in the world who would have done anything to harm Jimmy, I'm totally baffled by his behavior. What do you think, Laura?"

Laura was quiet for several moments, seemingly in a world of her own. Her eyes were closed as if she didn't want any distractions. Finally, she began to speak. "I think something is going on in that house and Patron senses it. I'm not getting anything about you being in danger, and the fact that he didn't growl or bark tells me he agrees, that you weren't in any danger."

"So why do you think his hackles were up?" Marty asked.

"First, answer this for me. You kind of indicated that he was focused on Horace. What about Ruby? Did you notice his hackles going up when she was speaking or interacting with you?"

Marty thought for a moment and then said, "No, now that I think about it, it was only when Horace was talking. Do you think Horace is somehow involved in all of this? But how could that be? He loved Jimmy like a brother."

"I don't know, but if Patron thinks something is off with Horace, you can pretty much take it to the bank that something is going on."

John stopped the conversation by saying, "I better get dinner ready. Jeff has done such a number on the appetizers, the rest of you barely had a chance for any, and I'm sure you're starving. Give Max and me a few minutes and dinner will be served. Jeff, we all want to hear what you found out, but don't start until Max and I get back."

CHAPTER SEVENTEEN

Fifteen minutes later Max and John returned with the cod, Brussel sprouts in a sauce, a fruit salad, and a loaf of warm sourdough bread.

Everyone was quiet while they ate, with Jeff being the first to speak. "John, I don't know how you do it. If my mother had ever told me she was serving cod and Brussel sprouts for dinner, I would have told her I couldn't eat, because the coach had scheduled a late practice, and I'd grab something later on. Seriously, this was excellent. Max, John, my compliments."

Everyone agreed with Jeff's assessment of dinner and then John said, "Okay, I think we have sufficient sustenance in us to continue the discussion about the death of Jimmy Joseph. Marty left off with one of the suspects having a pretty rock-solid alibi. Jeff, what did you find out?"

"I wish I could say I spent the whole day working on it. Unfortunately, the reality is that one of the murdered young people at the music festival is the son of the mayor of Palm Springs. Trust me, I spent most of the day placating my police chief who's getting all kinds of flak from the mayor and other elected officials to find the murderer. The mayor also had the senator, the assemblyman, and the Congressman who represent Palm Springs call me and tell me they expected me to find the killer."

"That's tough, man," Les said. "Do you have any leads in the case?"

"Not a darned one. I know the Joseph case is important because of his status. Yet, one of the victims at the music festival is the mayor's son, and trust me, it's kind of like a gnat on an elephant, the music festival murders being the elephant. I did assign one of my men to run checks on the other suspects to see what would come up and here's what he found.

"I'll start with Jimmy's sister, Eva. She's squeaky clean, not even a parking ticket. Her son, however, is another matter. He's had a number of brushes with the law. Nothing really big, but there's definitely a pattern of breaking the law such as hit and runs, although no one was hurt, just the cars, petty theft, and domestic violence. He's never done any time, but he's no choir boy."

"Do you think Jimmy knew that and that's why he wouldn't give his sister the money," Les asked.

"Have no idea, and I probably never will, but I'm guessing Jimmy knew what a bad apple his nephew was. The next one on the list is his manager, Randy. Just as Marty's been told, he's been a marrying fool, and paid dearly for each one. The check my guy ran showed he was seriously in debt, so that certainly could be a motive. He lives in Vegas, as does Jimmy's nephew. The first thing I need to do is find out where both of them were yesterday."

He turned towards Marty. "I haven't had a chance to thank you for talking to Jimmy's people and the neighbor today. The house is still off-limits for an appraisal, so I was kind of hoping you could spend tomorrow doing a little investigative work for me. I was able to get phone numbers and addresses for the other four suspects, that is, if you're game."

"Sure, happy to help. I'll see what I can find out," Marty said.

"Tell you what. I'll make time tomorrow morning to call a friend of mine who's on the police force in Las Vegas. I did a big favor for him a little while back, and I can call in that chit. He could probably have one of his men check out the whereabouts of Jimmy's nephew and his manager and see if they have alibis that will stick."

"Okay, that's three of the five people on the suspect list," Marty said. "What about the other two, the rejected fan, and the performer who's no longer at the Red Velvet Lounge?"

"I have addresses and telephone numbers for them. They both live in Palm Springs and have clean records. Other than that, I don't have anything more, but I do have a request for you."

"What's the request?"

"I'd like Patron to be with you if you decide to go to anyone's home or office. I have a lot of faith in that dog, and we both know, as attached as he is to you, he'd do whatever is needed to protect you."

"Yes, I can do that. Matter of fact, I think he likes going places with me." She turned to Laura. "Speaking of Patron, any last thoughts on his behavior earlier today?"

"No, nothing is coming to me, but I do agree with Jeff. Keep him with you. I know this is going to sound silly, but I've found if I put a problem in my mind right before I go to sleep, when I wake up the next morning the answer is there. It's as if something visited my mind in the middle of the night and solved whatever problem I was having. I'll put Patron and his behavior in there tonight and see what I come up with."

"Thanks, Laura. I'll be waiting with bated breath," she said with a grin. "No seriously, I really am curious, and even though I kid you about this, there is no doubt in my mind that you have powers or some kind of something or other that the rest of us don't have."

Marty turned towards the others sitting at the table, "Since it looks like I have to do some serious sleuthing tomorrow, think I'll call it a night. Jeff, are you about ready?"

"Yes, it's going to be a very early morning for me. You go on in, and I'll take the dogs out one last time. Duke, Patron, let's go." He stood up from the table and headed for the gate, the dogs in step behind him.

Laura and Les helped Max and John clear the table and within minutes the courtyard was dark and silent. The only sound was that of the gate opening as Jeff returned with the dogs.

CHAPTER EIGHTEEN

Marty rolled over the following morning and found that Jeff's side of the bed was empty. She listened for a moment, but the house was quiet. She looked at the clock on the nightstand which read 6:30 a.m.

I guess he wasn't kidding when he said he was going into work early, she thought as she stretched and yawned. *That means he had to get up about 5:30. Hope he had some breakfast. From what he said last night, today was going to be a difficult one for him. Poor guy. Hope I'll be able to help him.*

She got out of bed and walked into the kitchen where she was met by two very friendly dogs who were more than ready to have their breakfast.

Well, at least he ate. I can tell from the dishes in the sink and the coffee's still on, so he must have taken a little time for himself. And here's the paper spread out on the kitchen table. Hope he had time to read the comics and the sports page, his favorites.

As she looked at the paper, she recoiled when she saw the headline on the front page. In large letters on the upper right, above the fold, it read "Mayor's Son Murdered Police Dragging Their Feet." The article ran two columns down the length of the front page and continued on page three, where it took up a full page.

Poor Jeff, she thought. *From the looks of this, he is definitely not going to have a good day. I need to do everything I can to help him with the Joseph case.*

She fed the dogs, showered, dressed, and then sat down at the kitchen table with a toasted bagel while she read the newspaper article. Jeff's name appeared in it several times and not always in a complimentary way.

When she'd finished reading the paper, she went into her office and got a notebook out of her desk. For the next hour she wrote down everything she knew about the murder of Jimmy Joseph. She even wrote down the name of Carla McIntyre, only so she'd have something to cross off. It made her feel better.

She hadn't touched base with Carl since she'd taken him back to his shop on the day of the murder. Since he was helping her with the appraisal, it was only fair that she let him know what was going on. The store opened at 9:00, so he should be in by now, she reasoned. She punched in his number on her cell phone.

"Palm Springs Antique Shoppe, this is Carl, may I help you?" the voice on the other end of the phone said.

"Good morning, Carl. It's Marty. I thought I'd bring you up to date on the appraisal and Jimmy Joseph."

"I heard he died, if that's why you're calling. You kind of promised me that this appraisal wouldn't have any murders attached to it, so I was glad when the newscaster I was watching just said he'd died, not that he'd been murdered. If he'd said that I don't know what I would have done," Carl said.

"Uh, Carl, I hate to be the one to burst your balloon, but the coroner has determined that he was murdered, evidently by a poison called ricin."

It was very quiet on the other end of the phone, then Carl said, "Swell, that's just swell, Marty. Can't we have at least one appraisal where someone hasn't been murdered or is murdered while we're doing the appraisal? Marty, not only is this getting really old, I'm getting way too old for these murders. I really think this may be the last appraisal I ever agree to do with you."

"Carl, I understand how you feel, but you know that I never would knowingly take on an appraisal where someone was going to be murdered. Honestly, this was completely out of my control. Carl, I value your knowledge. Please reconsider and tell me you'll work with me again. There have just been a few occurrences which defy the laws of probability."

"Tell me one thing. What did that psycho sister of yours have to say about all of this?"

"She's psychic, not a psycho. Anyway, she had absolutely nothing to say. Here's what I've learned so far and Laura's only thought was about Patron and how he didn't think I was in any danger."

Marty told him about her meeting with Ruby and Horace and the list of five possible suspects that had been identified. Then she told him about how she'd talked to the neighbor next door to the Joseph property and how much she hated Jimmy's Mexican Fan Palms.

"Well, there you go, Marty. She'd have a perfect opportunity to murder him. All she had to do was wait outside her property, hide a little gun in a coat pocket, and shoot him with the ricin when he turned around to go back to his house after he'd gotten his mail. Case solved. Maybe I should give up antiques and become a detective."

"Carl, I wouldn't quit your day job quite yet if I were you. As a matter of fact, she has a rock-solid alibi for where she was when Jimmy was murdered. She was trying out for a role in a movie in Los Angeles. She said she can easily come up with a number of people who will vouch for her. I believed her. She said her agent was on his way to her home with the contract for her to sign. I don't think she'd make something up like that."

"That's easy enough to find out. I'm kind of a closet celebrity worshipper and there's this website that gives out all the information on who gets what roles in what movies. All that kind of stuff. Matter of fact it's kind of a 24/7 thing. I pay a subscription fee for it and they have someone available to answer any of your questions. Give me her name, and I'll see what I can find out for you."

"That would be great. I'm sure it's legit, but a backup would be nice. Her name is Carla McIntyre. Ring a bell?"

"As a matter of fact, it does. She was quite the darling of the movie crowd about twenty years ago, although I don't recall seeing her in any movies for a long time. Nobody's in the shop right now, so I'll do a little research on her and get right back to you."

"That would be great, Carl, I owe you one."

"Think you've got that wrong. You owe me a lot more than one for what I've been through with you. You're probably responsible for taking at least ten years off of my life."

"Carl, that's a little harsh, don't you think?"

"Well, maybe. I will give you one thing, no two. First, the appraisals I do with you are never dull and secondly, you provide me with some great stories when I'm at a cocktail party."

"I just try to be of help, Carl."

"I'm sure you do. I'll get right back to you."

CHAPTER NINETEEN

Later that morning, there was a knock on Marty's door and she heard Laura say, "Marty, it's me. Can I come in?"

"Of course. You know you're always welcome," Marty said as she opened the screen door. "Isn't it about time for you to leave for work?"

"Yes, but I wanted to talk to you before I left."

"Uh-oh, whenever you want to talk to me, it worries me. Am I to assume you had some night visitation regarding Patron's behavior yesterday?"

"As a matter of fact, I did," she said as she walked over to where the coffee pot was and poured herself a cup. She leaned back against the kitchen counter and said, "I don't have much to tell you. All I got were three words." She paused as she took a sip of her coffee.

"And?" Marty asked. "Are you going to be coy or tell me what the three words were?"

"Act of mercy."

"That's it. Those were the three words?"

"Yes. I woke up this morning and they kept running through my mind. I had a feeling of sadness rather than the danger feeling I've always had in the past."

"Did anything else come to you? Was I involved?" Marty asked.

"Yes, the words were in the foreground and you were in the background. That's all that came to me."

"So, I have Patron with hackles up and those three words. Oh, and I almost forgot. The mailbox."

"Yes, that's the extent of it. Although from what you and Jeff told us last night, looks like the mailbox was somehow related to his death. At least he was murdered when he went to get his mail. Anyway, I know it's not much to go on, but if I were analyzing Patron's behavior and the words that came to me, and there had been a murder involved, I'd say it wasn't a killing of revenge or hatred, but rather an act of mercy."

"Laura, it's like you're speaking in tongues. That's absolutely no help to me, and I don't see any nexus between your dream or whatever you call it, and the people on the suspect list. All of them had a reason why they wanted Jimmy dead. None of their possible motives fits with an act of mercy."

"I couldn't agree more, Marty, and I wish I had more for you, but I simply don't. The good news is I don't think you're in any kind of danger."

"Well, thank the Lord for small miracles, but that still doesn't get me any closer to finding out who killed Jimmy."

"Sorry, Sis. That's the best I can do. Thanks for the coffee, but I really do have to get to work. Anything you want me to tell Dick?"

"Yes. I'm sure he's well-aware of Jimmy's death. I left a message with Dick's secretary, after Jimmy was taken to the hospital, that we were unable to finish the appraisal. I said we'd resume when we could. Jeff told me that the house is still yellow-taped and off-limits due to the ongoing criminal investigation, but I'd expect we could resume tomorrow or the day after.

"Based on past experience, Dick's always wanted me to finish the appraisal of the decedent's estate because the value has to be known for estate purposes as well as insurance purposes. Unless I hear otherwise from him, I'm going to assume the same thing applies in this case, but why don't you find out if he's talked to Jimmy's lawyer about it?"

"Will do. If anything else comes to me, I'll let you know."

"Believe me, I'd really appreciate it if you would."

Just as Laura walked out the door, Marty's cell phone rang. She looked at the screen and saw it was Carl. "Thanks for getting back to me, Carl, what did you find out?"

"She told you the truth. She was hired to play the part of the mother of the lead actress. It's a nice role for her, actually it's a plum role. There were over one hundred women who read for the part. The fact that she got it tells me she'll probably be in demand from now on. She's never played the part of an older woman, and who knows, it could be the harbinger of a reboot of her career."

"Well, that means I can cross her off as one of the suspects for sure. Thanks Carl, I appreciate you finding out about her for me."

"Marty, you mentioned something about Miles Reed. I'm sorry, but I got distracted by a customer who was standing at the window looking in. Would you run that by me again?"

"Sure. Miles Reed used to play at the Red Velvet Lounge. The Lounge hired Jimmy after his heart attack and replaced Miles with Jimmy. From what I was told, Miles tried to get the owner of the Velvet to let him play there some other night during the week, but he refused, which meant Miles could no longer work there. Ring a bell?"

"Sure does. Some friends and I went to the Red Velvet Lounge before Jimmy took over and heard Miles Reed. He is really, really good. As a matter of fact, I remember we had a discussion afterwards about why he wasn't playing in Las Vegas. He seemed to be too good for Palm Springs. Are you going to talk to him?"

"Actually, I'm thinking about doing it this afternoon. I want to see if I can talk to the fan, Priscilla Simpson, this morning as well as Jimmy's sister. That would just leave me with Miles and Jimmy's agent, Randy. Why?"

"Well, you know I'm kinda' starstruck. I'd love a chance to talk to Miles, I mean, he was really that good. Mind if I tag along?"

"Carl, I'm shocked. I thought you didn't want anything to do with murders ever again. At least that's the impression I got."

"Well, Marty, I've been thinking. Maybe I was a little hasty in what I said about never appraising with you again. I have to say that the appraisals are always interesting, but I just don't want to be the one who makes them interesting, if you get what I mean."

"I think you're telling me you don't want to be the victim of some murderer when we're out on an appraisal. Would that about sum it up?"

"That it would. If you can assure me that I won't be, I'll take back what I said earlier about not appraising with you again."

"Carl, you know I can't absolutely promise you that. I mean, think about it. A crazed murderer could crash in through the windows looking for something, and we might just be in the wrong place at the wrong time. See what I mean?"

"I'm getting the sense you're somewhat of a fatalist, like if it's your time, it's your time. Is that about right?"

"Yes, although I would prefer you didn't use the word fatalist in describing me. I prefer to think of myself as an optimist, but I'm also pragmatic. We can't plan for every eventuality that might take place in the world, but I can promise you I'll do something that will make you happy."

"And what would that be?"

"I'll make sure that Patron is always with us when we do an appraisal. You remember how he alerted you when we were doing the woman's home who was donating her collection to the museum she was going to build. And when that didn't work out, her home became the museum and I was appointed the interim museum director."

"From your lips to God's ear. Promise me Patron will always be with us, and I'll be happy to help you,"

"Done."

"Good. Now about Miles. Are you planning on just showing up or are you going to make an appointment with him?"

"I thought I'd just show up. Jeff gave me his address. Evidently he's taken a job at some lounges here in the area, but I figure he won't be going there until later tonight. Why don't I pick you up about 2:00 this afternoon and we'll see what happens?"

"Can I bring my autograph book, 'cuz that guy is definitely going places, and his autograph might be really valuable in a few years."

"Carl, need I remind you that we're going to talk to him about a murder? If he's the killer, he'll be going places, but not the places where his autograph will be worth much."

"You've got a point." Carl was quiet for a few moments and then said, "Well, I think I'll see if I can get his autograph anyway. If he does turn out to be the killer, I'll just put it in the trash. If not, I may be a rich man."

"And I thought I was an optimist," Marty said. "See you at 2:00."

CHAPTER TWENTY

"Patron, come. We have some work to do," Marty said to the big white boxer who eagerly ran to her side. "We have to visit two women, pick up Carl, and go see a guy. Are you up for that, big boy?"

Patron arfed joyfully while she snapped his leash on him. She turned to Duke and said, "Duke, we'll be back this afternoon. I texted Les to take you for a walk when he takes a break from painting. Be good." She closed the gate behind them and she and Patron got in her car.

She'd used her Waze app to get the directions to the apartment where Priscilla lived. It was in an older part of Palm Springs that had lost its appeal to the people who had come to the desert in the last twenty years and expanded the original small town of Palm Springs much farther east.

Rancho Mirage, Palm Desert, and La Quinta were just a few of the far more desirable places for people to live while they played golf and enjoyed the warmth of the sun after dealing with the effects of winter in the northern United States and Canada. It wasn't called a playground for the rich and famous for nothing.

After the thirty-minute drive from the compound to the Palm Springs area, she pulled up to the curb in front of an apartment building that was long past its prime. Weeds grew where lush grass had once been planted. The sidewalk leading up to the door was cracked and paint was peeling off of the front door. Straggly succulents stood next to the front steps, succulents that were meant to thrive in the desert, but clearly lacked any attention being given to them.

"Okay, Patron. It's show time. I promised Jeff you'd be part of the investigation and so you are. Please be on your best behavior. Even though you're white and people usually like white dogs, some of them are put off by big dogs."

There were almost no cars on the street as is often the case in a blue-collar neighborhood where everyone is at work during the day. Marty would have been surprised if there had been a lot of parked cars. Clearly, this was an area where people survived, rather than thrived.

They walked in the front door of the building and entered a small vestibule. Next to the elevator was a roster of the residents. Priscilla Simpson lived in Apartment 2D on the second floor. They rode the elevator up to the second floor and walked down the hall to Priscilla's apartment. Marty rang the doorbell.

Marty wasn't sure what she was going to say to Priscilla if she was there. She thought she'd wing it, but now she was regretting not having prepared something.

A moment later a voice on the other side of the door asked, "Who is it?"

"My name is Marty Morgan, Priscilla. I'd like to talk to you about Jimmy Joseph. I'm his representative."

The door swung open and a woman stood there, her face swollen and black and blue. She looked at Marty and said, "It's about time he apologized or sent someone to apologize for him. Course now that he's dead, I guess it doesn't matter."

Marty didn't know what to say. She knew she was staring at the woman's face but she couldn't help it. Finally, she said, "I'd like to come in rather than discuss it here in the hallway. Would that be okay with you?"

"Are you going to bring that dog in here if I let you in?" Priscilla asked, looking down at Patron who was quite calm. That was one of the reasons Marty had wanted to bring Patron, in addition to promising Jeff that she would. She wanted to see what his response was to the people she was going to talk to. From what she was observing, if she were a betting woman, she'd bet that Priscilla wasn't the murderer.

"Yes, he goes wherever I go. I know it's silly, but I just like to have him with me. I really can't explain it. I hope you don't mind. He's quite well-behaved."

"All right. Come in and say what you have to say. As you can tell from my face, I've definitely felt better, and the doctor told me to take it very easy for the next few days."

Priscilla held the door open for them and Patron and Marty entered the small apartment. Marty looked past Priscilla and gasped. Every wall was covered from floor to ceiling with pictures of Jimmy Joseph. She'd never seen anything like it and was totally at a loss of words.

"Sit down, and yes, those are all pictures of Jimmy Joseph. I've lived with them for so long it's hard for me to take them down, but now that I've decided to make a new life for myself, I will."

Marty didn't know where to begin. Should she question Priscilla about her face and her reference to a doctor? Or should she say something about the pictures? Or maybe why she was there? She decided anything was better than the silence between them.

"You mentioned a doctor. Are you ill?"

"No, you can see for yourself why I'm under the care of a doctor.

I know my face doesn't look very good right now, but he promises it will when the swelling and the black and blue marks are gone."

"Did something happen to you?" Marty asked.

"You might say that. That something is called a scalpel or laser. I had a complete face lift. As a matter of fact, I got out of the hospital yesterday afternoon. I didn't heal quite as fast as the doctor wanted me to, so he kept me in an extra day. I was there three days, rather than the normal two."

"You must be so excited. I have a number of friends who have had face lifts and all of them are glad they did."

"It was nothing I'd planned on, but after I heard what that man said about me at the Red Velvet Lounge when I tried to get in to see Jimmy Joseph, I thought it was time. I've been ugly all my life, and I know it. But I never expected to hear someone else call me ugly and tell Jimmy he didn't need to see me because I was ugly. Nothing has ever hurt me that badly.

"Is that why you're here, to apologize to me on behalf of Jimmy? Because if you are, it's too late. These pictures of Jimmy are coming down as soon as I feel up to it. I've got a new face, and I'm starting a new life."

"No, I didn't come here to apologize to you. I'm sorry for what happened at the Red Velvet Lounge, but I'm here to see if you know anyone who would have wanted to kill Jimmy? When you were at the lounge that night, did you notice anything unusual?"

Priscilla was quiet for several moments and then she said, "You said kill Jimmy. The news report I saw on television said he'd died. I assumed he'd had another heart attack, but that wasn't the reason for his death, is that what you're saying?"

"He died from a poison called ricin. Evidently someone shot him with a pellet that had the poison in it. He died a few hours later in the hospital."

"I didn't know that. I'm sorry." She looked over at Marty with tears in her eyes. "Jimmy wasn't the one who said I was ugly. It was one of his people at the Red Velvet. I guess everything in my life really is changing. My facelift. Jimmy murdered. This is all a lot to take in."

"I'm sorry. The police department is deliberately not releasing the cause of death."

"Thank you. You said you were representing Jimmy. In what capacity?"

"My husband is the head detective at the Palm Springs Police Department. I've helped him with several cases in the past that have involved people I knew. I'm an antique appraiser and was conducting an appraisal at Jimmy's home the day he was murdered. Unfortunately, the same day there were also several murders at the music festival, one of whom was the mayor's son.

"You can't imagine the pressure being brought to bear on my husband by politicians and others to find the murderer. I'm trying to help him with a little legwork by talking to people who knew Jimmy. His right-hand man had your card and was getting ready to put it into a fan database when he was murdered. Jimmy had handed him the card when he was at the Red Velvet, and I thought maybe you might know something."

Well, that's not exactly how it went down, Marty thought, *but given the circumstances, I think a little fib here and there will be okay. Nothing I just said will hurt Priscilla.*

"No, I know nothing other than what I told you earlier about hearing someone say that I was really ugly. I've had a little time to think about it, actually a lot of time while I was in the hospital, and I think it may have been a blessing in disguise. Before I made the decision to have the facelift, quite frankly I'd thought about doing something to hurt Jimmy the way I'd been hurt. Finally, I had to admit that even though it was one of Jimmy's people, it wasn't Jimmy, so it was time for me to give up my anger at him as well."

"How so?" Marty asked.

"I used my ugliness to keep me from developing any friendships or other personal relationships. I stuffed any desires I might have had for a normal life down and consoled myself with pictures of Jimmy and telling myself that I was his number one fan. Before my mother died, she told me what I was doing was really unhealthy. She told me that she was leaving me quite an inheritance, and she wanted me to use it to make a better life for myself. Instead, I played the martyr, put the inheritance into a mutual fund, and surrounded myself with Jimmy. I never touched my inheritance.

"I have a master's degree in tax law, but I always felt as ugly as I was, no one would ever hire me. I took a menial job with an insurance company that I could do here at home, so I would rarely have to go out of my apartment and interact with people. I had my groceries delivered and bought whatever I needed online. The words I heard at the Red Velvet that night have changed my life."

"I decided my mother was right. My attitude towards life was distinctly unhealthy. I contacted my broker, took a lot of money out of my account, and decided to start with a face lift. Then I made a down payment on a condominium in La Quinta. Once I get settled there, I'm going to begin interviewing for a job using my degree."

"It sounds like you've planned this very carefully."

"I'd like to think so. I understand that private banking has become a big deal with a lot of the banks and investment companies. As much money as there is in Palm Springs and with a much older population, I would think skills like mine would be desirable. Plus, I graduated magna cum laude from both college and law school. That should count for something."

"While I'm in the process of moving into the condo and seeking employment, I'm also going to treat myself to learning how to apply makeup, go to the best hair stylist I can find, get a personal trainer, and spend some serious time getting to know the personal shoppers at the best stores in the area."

"I wish you luck, Priscilla. I'm sorry that it took the horrible experience you went through at the Red Velvet to start all this, but like you said, maybe it was a blessing in disguise.

"It's funny. My mother begged me to go see a plastic surgeon, but I always refused. I thought if I looked better it might result in someone wanting to have a relationship with me and I was afraid. I didn't want to set myself up for a relationship failure. Looking the way I did resulted in a pretty awful childhood and teen years. I'd learned to accept the fact that people thought I had agorophobia. Actually, I didn't. I just didn't want to be around people because I knew they could hurt me.

"I'm sure wherever my mother is, she's pretty happy about the way this turned out. Actually, she might have arranged for it to happen," Priscilla said with a laugh. "Before this, I never would have let you in. I guess I'm ready to let in all kinds of new experiences. On one hand, I'm terrified, and on the other, I'm terribly excited."

"It sounds like you don't have a lot of friends."

"That might be the understatement of the year. I have none, zero, zip, nada. I'd never let anyone get that close to me even if they wanted to, although I have to admit, they weren't breaking down the door to get to me."

"What I was going to say is that I'd love to get together with you for lunch after you get all your ducks in a row," Marty said. "I live about a half hour from Palm Springs, but I'm usually here in town at least once a week, sometimes more often. I mean it. Please, give me a call. Here's my phone number," Marty said as she jotted it down on a piece of paper and handed it to Priscilla.

With that she stood up and said, "I've taken enough of your time, Priscilla. You need to heal and think about all the wonderful things that are just about ready to happen to you. I'll be sending friendly thoughts to you. Goodbye."

"Thank you for your offer of friendship. I don't think anyone has offered that to me before. I'm touched. I'll be calling."

When Marty and Patron were back in the car she said, "Well, that was interesting. What a story. If all else fails, she can write a book about her life. It would probably become a bestseller. Rags to riches, ugly to beautiful. She'll probably end up marrying some gazillionaire and live happily ever after in some McMansion. Sure never thought that's what we'd learn when we started out today. However, that's one more name crossed off the list of possible suspects. Now on to Eve."

CHAPTER TWENTY-ONE

Eve lived very close to Priscilla's apartment. In fact, the apartments could have been interchangeable. Same era, same maintenance or lack thereof, same tired feeling to it. Marty wondered if they'd been built by the same developer. The sidewalk even looked the same.

When she and Patron walked into the building and checked the roster posted next to the elevator, she saw that Eve Wright lived in apartment 1D. Jeff had been able to get her work schedule from the restaurant where she worked, so Marty was hopeful she'd be home.

When they reached her apartment, the door was slightly ajar, and Marty said in a loud voice, "Hello. Mrs. Wright, are you in there?"

A moment later a middle-aged woman with brown hair flecked with grey walked through the small living room to the door and said, "I'm Mrs. Wright. What can I do for you?"

"My name's Marty Morgan. I wondered if I could talk to you for a few minutes. It's about your brother, Jimmy Joseph."

"And you're with?" she asked.

"Unofficially the police department. I often help one of the detectives when that department gets overloaded which happens to be the case right now because of the triple homicide that occurred at the music festival. This is in regards to your brother's death. First of all, my condolences. Even though he'd had a heart attack, that still doesn't prepare one for a sudden unexpected death."

"No, it doesn't. Come in Marty. I take it your bringing your dog with you?"

"Yes, he pretty much goes everywhere I go."

Eve gestured toward two worn armchairs in the living room. Marty was struck by the vast difference between where Eve lived and where Jimmy had lived. It was like night and day.

"How can I help you?" Eve asked.

"I don't know if you've been told, but your brother was murdered. The police have not released the news yet, hoping that the person who committed the murder will do something to reveal themselves."

A number of emotions flickered across Eve's face as Marty told her of Jimmy's murder – fear, anger, guilt. All of which were gone in an instant.

"I'm not only here to offer my condolences, as well as the police department's, but also to ask if you can think of anyone who might have killed Jimmy? Did he ever say anything to you about someone he was having problems with?"

Eve was quiet for several moments and then she stood up and walked over to the window. Her back faced Marty as she said, "My brother and I were not close. I'm sure you'd find that out one way or another. You see, my family hated my husband. Dad and Jimmy always thought my mother died because of a broken heart and my marriage was what caused it."

She turned around, walked back to her chair, and sat down. "Because of that I became estranged from my family. In fact, I haven't seen Jimmy in years. The last time may have been at my father's funeral, but even then there was so much tension between us

I think we may have said hello to each other and that was it."

"It must have been hard for you to see Jimmy rise to fame and you weren't able to be a part of his inner circle or congratulate him on his accomplishments," Marty said.

"Actually, what was harder was to see what his accomplishments had brought him in the way of money, like the way he lived and his home. Several times I drove by it comparing it to this tenement-like apartment I live in. Jimmy and my parents had been right. My husband was a real loser. He left me in the dead of the night with a small child and no money. I divorced him, but the years have not been easy for me, as you can see. I have to work two jobs just to maintain this dumpy apartment."

"Did you ever ask Jimmy for help?" Marty asked.

"No. I was too proud, and he never offered. Once he told me he had left me something in his trust, but that was the only time money was discussed. I've often thought it was his way of punishing me for marrying my husband, and in Jimmy's mind, causing my mother's death."

"You mentioned you haven't seen Jimmy in years. Have you talked to him?"

Again, emotions flitted across Eve's face. Marty was interested in what she was going to say, because she knew that Eve had spoken with Jimmy about a week before his death. If she said no, then she'd be lying, although Marty couldn't call her on it.

"No, I haven't talked to him in years. I have no idea if he's changed his trust, or if I'll even get anything from his estate. It's too bad when a brother and sister can't at least have a relationship where they call each other from time to time, but that's the way it was with the two of us. It's been years since I've talked to him, unfortunately."

Marty looked at Eve's hands which were tightly clasped in her lap, so tightly clasped her knuckles were showing white. She remembered

Jeff once saying every person who was trying to hide something had a tell, something they inadvertently did that revealed they were lying or guilty or whatever. Marty wondered whether Eve's tell was her tightly clasped hands.

"Eve, do you have any children?"

"Yes, I have a son, Mickey. He lives in Las Vegas and rarely gets to Palm Springs, unfortunately. I miss him."

"Since you and Jimmy weren't close, what about your son and Jimmy? There would be no reason for Jimmy not to see him."

Eve looked away and then back at Marty. "No, they never have been close. I wish they could have been, but Jimmy chose to have nothing to do with me or my family, and that included my son."

"What does your son do in Las Vegas, Eve?"

Her eyes darted all around the room as she tried to avoid eye contact with Marty. "He deals with finances. I'm really not sure. Mickey's always had a very good mind for figures, so doing things in that area was a natural for him."

Right, Marty thought, *I suppose gambling could be construed as doing something with figures, but that's a pretty big leap. Maybe that's how she justified his gambling, but if he was all that good at it, I rather doubt he'd need his mother to call his uncle to see if she could get money for him to keep him from being killed for not paying his gambling debts.*

"That's wonderful," Marty said in an upbeat voice. I've never been any good with figures and things of that nature. I think it's a gift. He's fortunate to have that ability."

"Yes, he is," Eve said.

"When do you plan on seeing him again?" Marty asked. "With so little family, it must be hard on you not to be able to see him more."

"It is, but I really don't know. He's very busy in Las Vegas, and with my jobs, I can't take time off to visit him. Oh well, we'll work it out somehow. You'll have to excuse me for cutting this short, but I need to get ready for work. I hope what I told you helped, although there wasn't much."

You helped me more than you'll ever know, Marty thought. *You just lied about your son and the only reason you'd do that is to cover for him. You've just succeeded in moving him up to number one on my suspect list.*

"You were very helpful. I'm just sorry I have to be here under these circumstances. Thanks for taking the time to see me. Let's go, Patron."

After Marty left Eve's apartment, she and Patron walked down the sidewalk to her car. Patron was perfectly calm, hackles unraised.

Well, based on Patron's response to Eve, Marty thought, *I'm pretty sure I can cross her off the list, not that she was ever a high priority suspect, but her son, that's an entirely different matter. I need to call Jeff. Maybe they could get someone from the police department to go to Las Vegas and interview him or have the Las Vegas Police Department bring him in for questioning.*

CHAPTER TWENTY-TWO

Marty had packed a lunch for herself and a dog food snack for Patron before she'd left the compound earlier that morning. She had a little time before she was scheduled to pick Carl up at his shop and decided to drive to a nearby park where she could walk Patron and they could both have something to eat. It would also give her an opportunity to call Jeff and tell him how Eve had lied to her.

After Patron finished his bowl of dog food, he promptly stretched out in the warm sun and fell sleep. While he was eating Marty enjoyed the large salad she'd packed. She would have preferred to go to In N' Out again, but an inner voice had warned her if she started going there regularly, she'd have to get a second job to pay for the new wardrobe her weight gain would require.

When she was finished, she took her cell phone out of her purse and called Jeff. He answered on the first ring. "Marty, I was just getting ready to call you. Oh, excuse me a minute." She heard him telling someone in his office that he'd be there in five minutes and to please close the door on their way out.

When he got back on the phone he said, "Marty you wouldn't believe the day I'm having. Turns out the mayor's son was selling drugs at the concert. We had an undercover officer there who had bought drugs from him right before he was murdered when a drug deal he was involved in went bad. That's why his two friends were murdered as well."

"Oh Jeff, I can't imagine the firestorm that must be bringing to your department."

"I'm sure you can't. The press got wind of it and the whole morning has been a juggling act of press, politicians, and the mayor trying to squelch the story. He's called a news conference for 3:00 this afternoon, and the talk is he's going to resign his position as mayor. This has got to be one of the most grueling days I've ever spent."

"Oh, honey. I'm so sorry. At least I can brighten your day with my news."

"Shoot. It couldn't come at a better time."

"I've solved the Jimmy Joseph murder case," she said proudly.

"You've what?" Jeff asked in a loud voice.

"I said I've solved the Jimmy Joseph case. I'm almost certain that Mickey Wright, Jimmy Joseph's nephew, murdered him." She went on to tell him about her meeting with Mickey's mother and how she'd lied to Marty. "I'm sure she was lying to cover up for her son. You need to have one of your men or maybe a Las Vegas detective question him."

"Oh, Marty. I hate to burst your happy bubble and do away with your good news, but Mickey is the reason I was getting ready to call you. You see, I just had a telephone call from my contact in Las Vegas. I called him first thing this morning and Mickey was already on his radar for a number of things."

"So what's the problem?"

"The problem is that Mickey was in jail in Las Vegas the day that Jimmy was murdered. That gives him an airtight alibi. He'd been arrested for being drunk and disorderly the night before, and it took him until this morning to get bail money so he could get out. There's no way he's the murderer. Sorry."

"Oh, dear. I wonder why his mother lied to me?"

"I'd bet she knew he was in jail and she was probably trying to get bail money for him. I'm sure she realizes what a bad apple he is and just didn't want him to have any more problems than he already has."

Marty was quiet for a few moments and then said, "Yes, that makes sense. It would be pretty hard to turn your son over to law enforcement authorities, no matter how you felt about the things he'd done. Kind of like the umbilical cord is still attached."

"Exactly, Marty. Listen, sorry to cut this call short, but I've got to go. I'm trying to keep the press from getting any more information until the mayor holds his press conference."

"One last thing, Jeff. Did your contact in Las Vegas mention anything about Jimmy's manager, Randy Allen?"

"No. He's still working on it. Sorry, Marty, I have to go now. See you tonight. Loves."

He ended the call and Marty looked at the phone for a moment before she put it in her purse. *Poor guy,* she thought. *Talk about being in a pressure cooker. When it involves politicians and the press, that's got to be brutal. Maybe I can find something out about Miles Reed when Carl and I go there this afternoon, although I have a feeling that's a long shot.*

She threw her trash in a nearby trash can, woke Patron up, and together they walked back to her car. A few minutes later she drove by Carl's shop, but couldn't find a parking place in front of it so she turned down a side street, parked, rolled the windows down slightly for Patron, and walked to the Palm Springs Antique Shoppe.

"Good afternoon, Danivs," she said to Carl's assistant. "How are you and Carl doing with the decorating arm of the business? When Carl told me he was concerned you'd be leaving the shop to open your own business, I suggested that he make it part of the antique shop. Seemed like a natural. I think it was a good decision."

"Marty, you wouldn't believe it. It was the most natural pairing in the world. Carl has the best antiques in Palm Springs. I do the home decorating with carte blanche to use items from the shop and everybody's happy. The clients love what I do. I make money and Carl makes money selling clients the things I decorate with. Kind of like a hand fitting in a glove. I'm so glad you suggested it to him. He knows everybody who's anybody in Palm Springs, so it was perfect. Thank you."

"I'm glad I was able to help. Speaking of Carl, we were supposed to meet here at 2:00."

"He'll be out in a minute. One of his better clients wants to buy a number of things from Carl as a gift for his daughter and son-in-law to be. He's on the phone with the man now giving him suggestions. Ah, speak of the devil," she said as Carl emerged from his office in the rear of the shop.

"Sorry, Marty, but that was one telephone call I had to take. I can close the shop and do nothing for the rest of the month with what that phone call just brought in. Let me get my autograph book and I'm ready to go."

"Carl, you were serious, weren't you? You're going to hit Miles up for an autograph, aren't you? This is downright embarrassing. He's going to think we're a couple of wackos."

"Speak for yourself, darling. Anyone who's in show biz loves to have someone ask them for their autograph. It's what they live for. You know, adulation by the masses. Now that Jimmy's dead, I wonder if I should show that Elvis jacket to him? I never was paid for it even though Jimmy said he wanted it."

"That's a moral dilemma I'll leave up to you. Please don't involve me in that."

"Okay," he said cheerfully, "I'm ready. Do you think I look okay?"

Marty had been looking at an early Dresden figurine and had barely looked up while she was talking to him. She set the figurine down and studied him before speaking. "Carl, you look great. You're one of the few men living in Palm Springs who can wear an ascot and not look silly. And the white suit with your tan is great. I'm sure Miles will be duly impressed."

"Thank you, sweetie, I try. I wanted to show him that I value what he does, so I dressed up a little. Figured he'd like it."

"I'm sure he'll feel honored."

Carl opened the door for her and they started walking to her car. "Actually, Carl, the pickings are getting slimmer." She told him about Carla, Priscilla, Eve, and Mickey. "The only other two left on my suspect list are Miles and Jimmy's agent, Randy Allen. If it turns out to be neither one of them, I will have hit a block wall and with what Jeff is dealing with at the moment, it's the last thing he needs."

"What is he dealing with?" Carl asked as they got in her car. He reached back to pet Patron whose whole body was wiggling in joy at seeing Carl.

"Oh, just that the mayor's son who was murdered was dealing drugs at the concert, that the press and politicians are camped out in Jeff's office, and that the mayor is holding a press conference at 3:00, probably to resign."

Carl's hand reached for his phone in his pocket and Marty immediately put her hand on top of his. "Don't even think about it, Carl. I know you're the disseminator and main conduit for any news that happens in Palm Springs, but this was told to me in confidence by a law enforcement person, and it is to stay confidential, a word I know is not very prevalent in your vocabulary.

While Carl loved his antiques, the one thing he treasured more than anything was good gossip, and what Marty had just told him was some of the best he'd recently heard.

It's a shame I can't let people know what's happening, he thought, *but after our meeting with Miles I might even have better gossip. Since I'll be sitting in on whatever happens there, it won't be gossip, it will be the truth.*

"Marty, my lips are sealed," he said, making a motion of locking his lips. "Upward and on to meet with Miles. I'm so excited I can hardly stand it."

CHAPTER TWENTY-THREE

Miles Reed lived in the guesthouse of a large home in the old Palm Springs area. It was located behind a pink stucco house with a matching colored half stucco wall topped by tiles. The guesthouse repeated the same theme with a heavily tiled swimming pool separating them. Marty, Carl, and Patron walked down the driveway to the guesthouse and rang the bell. Marty was encouraged that there was a car in the driveway. She hoped it meant Miles was home.

"Coming," a voice said from inside. A moment later the door was opened by a man in his early forties dressed in a light beige short-sleeved shirt, matching chinos, and dark brown tasseled moccasins. He was deeply tanned with jet black hair which was beginning to grey at the temples.

"May I help you?" he asked, looking down at Patron.

"Yes," Marty said. "My name is Marty Malone. This is Carl Jenkins, and the dog is Patron. He's pretty much my shadow. We'd like to talk to you about Jimmy Joseph. May we come in? I promise Patron is very well-behaved."

"Yes, but I don't understand why you want to talk to me. I don't have much time to talk," he said as he walked into his living room. "I have to catch a flight to Las Vegas." Out of the corner of her eye she noticed Carl nodding as he looked at the Native American rug on the tile floor. She assumed that meant Carl thought it was good.

"This won't take long Mr. Reed. My husband is a police detective who at the moment is overwhelmed by too many murders in the Palm Springs area. I was doing a personal property appraisal for Mr. Joseph the day he was murdered. Since my husband's department was overloaded, and I'd been in the home and gotten to know the people who worked with him, I told my husband I'd see if I could find out anything."

"So you're not here in an official capacity, is that correct? And you, sir, what is your involvement?" he asked as he turned and looked at Carl.

"Quite simply, Mr. Reed. I'm a huge fan of yours. I own the Palm Springs Antique Shoppe and was helping Marty with the appraisal of Jimmy's memorabilia collection, and like her, I was at Jimmy's home the day Jimmy was murdered. When she told me she was coming here, I asked if I could tag along."

"Wait a minute," Miles said, "I don't remember seeing anything on the news or in the paper about his death being caused by murder."

"That's true," Marty said. "The department hasn't released that information yet. There was speculation, but they wanted to keep it quiet while they investigated, however, with the other murders at the music festival, they're stretched a little thin at the moment."

"Yes, I heard about that. Three young people died. What a tragedy."

Marty could sense Carl was doing everything in his power not to tell Miles what Marty had told him about the deaths. She was certain if she hadn't been there, Miles would be well aware of information regarding the mayor and the mayor's son by now.

"If you can tell me anything about Jimmy Joseph, I'd appreciate it. I know that you used to play at the Red Velvet Lounge and then

Jimmy took over, and from what I've heard, a lot of people were sorry that you were no longer there. It must have been hard for you."

"I'd be lying if I said it wasn't hard at first. In fact, my brother even suggested if Jimmy wasn't around, that I could probably get my old job back. But I'm a Buddhist and with all the meditation I've done, and the retreats I've attended, I've learned that things generally happen for a reason. Actually, the Red Velvet replacing me with Jimmy turned out to be a godsend."

"That sounds quite provocative, Mr. Reed. I'd heard that you had talked to the owner of the Velvet about still playing there in addition to Jimmy, but he didn't want to do that."

"Yes, that's true. When he told me, I didn't know what I was going to do. He said he knew Jimmy's manager and he'd give him a call recommending that he talk to me about being my agent. I didn't think much about it, and I was able to get some short-term gigs playing at two other clubs in town. They're nowhere near the caliber of the Velvet, but they have decent enough crowds. I've developed a following in both of them in a rather short period of time."

"Maybe I'm missing something, but I still fail to see how losing your job at the Red Velvet turned out to be a blessing for you," Marty said.

"Over the weekend I got a call from Jimmy's manager, Randy Allen. The owner of the Velvet had called Randy and told him since Jimmy could no longer travel and the only place he was playing was at the Velvet, that he could probably use a new client. He recommended me highly. Randy asked me to go to Las Vegas and meet with him.

"When did you go?" Marty asked.

"I left the morning Jimmy was murdered. I spent the night there. If you're asking if I have an alibi, I certainly do. I have plane tickets, a hotel receipt, plus a number of people in Randy's office, and even where we went to lunch, can vouch for me. I treated Randy to lunch, so I even have a receipt for that. I was in Las Vegas the entire day that Jimmy was murdered."

"I hate to ask this of you, Mr. Reed, but would you mind showing them to me? I can tell the police department that there is no way you could be considered a suspect once I've seen those receipts."

"Certainly, now I'll tell you how this is a blessing, then I have to go. When I met with Randy, he asked me to audition for him. He did a demo tape of it and told me he was going to see if he could get any bites on it. He called late yesterday and told me that I would be opening for one of the largest stars in Las Vegas beginning tomorrow."

"Wow, I knew it. I just knew it," Carl said.

"What are you talking about?" Miles asked.

"When Marty told me your name, I remembered going to the Velvet and seeing you with some friends. Afterwards, we were all talking about how good you were and that you should be performing in Las Vegas, rather than Palm Springs. By the way, Mr. Reed, I brought my autograph book with me. Would you mind signing it for me?" Carl asked with a big smile as he reached into the satchel he always carried.

"Of course." He quickly wrote his signature and then said, "You can look at the receipts while I finish packing. My Uber driver will be here shortly." He walked into his bedroom and returned with the receipts, handing them to Marty.

She looked them over and said, "Looks perfectly good to me. And you were with Randy Allen all this time?"

"Yes. He actually picked me up at the airport at 9:30 and I was with him until he took me to my hotel that evening about 8:00. I hope all of this helps you."

"Very much. Thank you for your time and congratulations on

your success. I'll look forward to seeing your name in the papers and on the news. I wish you well," Marty said as she stood up and began walking towards the door, Carl by her side.

When they got in her car, Marty looked over at Carl who was beside himself with excitement. He looked like a football player who had just scored the winning touchdown on the last play of the game. "I knew it, I just knew it. This autograph is my most prized possession. I am so excited. I actually talked to the man who is going to replace Elvis and Elton John."

"Carl, I don't know if I'd go quite that far. They set a pretty high bar."

"Marty, if you'd heard him play like I did, you wouldn't be saying that."

"Well, I'm glad for him, but…"

"Oh, Marty. Oh no." Carl exclaimed, a look of horror on his face.

Marty looked at him, having no idea what was causing Carl's anguish. "Carl, what is it?"

"Marty, I missed my opportunity. I can't believe I was that starstruck," he said pounding his fist on his thigh.

"You've completely lost me. Care to fill me in?" she asked as she drove towards Carl's shop.

"The jacket. I never told him about the Elvis jacket. Maybe we should turn around, and I could show him the picture of it that I have on my phone."

"No. This is definitely not the right time. I think it would be much better if you sent a letter to him here at his house and enclose the picture of the jacket. Let him take the lead from there."

"But Marty, think how wonderful it would be if he could wear it tomorrow night. I mean it would cement his career. Elvis' jacket. What a way to start your career out and he'd be so indebted to me, he'd probably give me tickets to his show for life. You know, right on the front row, and I'll bet he'd give me a pass so I could go backstage after his shows. Then I could probably get to know all the other stars and they'd want to buy antiques from me. I could probably open an antique shop in Las Vegas. Of course, I'd have to move there. What do you think?"

"I think you need to take a deep breath and slow down, Carl. One jacket does not an antique shop in Las Vegas make. Start with the letter. One step at a time."

"Yeah, you're probably right, but this may be the most exciting day of my life."

"If you're that into stars, why wouldn't meeting Jimmy Joseph be your best day ever?"

"Because he was the setting sun. Miles is the rising star. It's like with him all things are possible. It's a new day. When the sun's setting, things are pretty much over, don't you agree?"

"I'll think about it, Carl. I'll think about it," she said as she shook her head and rolled her eyes back in a show of mock disbelief at Carl's antics.

CHAPTER TWENTY-FOUR

After she dropped Carl off at his shop and was driving back to the compound, Marty said, "You were great today, Patron. Not one bark or growl. That's the good news. The bad news is I guess that means none of the people we visited today are the murderer. Agreed?"

Patron let out a small woof and with his head between his paws, resumed sleeping in the back seat.

"Thought you'd agree with me. Thanks, Patron." All was quiet in the back seat.

A half hour later she pulled into the driveway of the compound and saw that all the residents, plus Max, were there, including Jeff. She got Patron out of the car, opened the gate so Duke could join them for a short walk in the desert. She watched them greet each other happily and then run a short distance into the surrounding desert, scattering desert life in their wake.

Marty called them to her and the three of them went back to the courtyard where her friends and husband were enjoying a glass of wine, catching up on the events of the day.

"Be with you in a minute. I need to change clothes, drop off these notes, and feed the starving beasts. Don't start anything interesting without me," she said with a laugh.

A few minutes later Marty, Duke, and Patron walked out of her house, the dogs calm and content after having been fed. They walked up to Jeff who willingly gave them ear scratches. They then completed a circle of the table, demanding the same from everyone.

Marty looked at her husband and said, "Jeff, I'm surprised you're home this early. I thought you were up to your neck in alligators, so to speak, and wouldn't be here until much later."

"I think alligators would have been easier than the politicians and the press, although I'm not sure that both of those groups wouldn't qualify as alligators. If you haven't heard it on the radio or television, let me be the first to tell you that we have an interim mayor in Palm Springs. It's come out that the mayor's son was a major drug dealer in Palm Springs and the mayor decided it would be prudent for him to resign before anyone called for his resignation."

"Wow," Les said. "I'll bet the press was all over that story. You couldn't make one up like that."

"It was like a feeding frenzy. The disgraced mayor was escorted away from City Hall by several members of Palm Spring's finest, my fellow law enforcement people. To make the whole thing even worse, the other two young men killed at the music festival, were all sons of prominent Palm Springs business people.

"Turns out when the drug deal went bad and the shooting started, it was the mayor's son who shot and killed the other two, but not before they fatally wounded him. A nearby security camera caught the whole shootout on tape, so that's what happened.

"Oh yeah, it was a great day. I finally said I'd had enough and left. Think it was Scarlett O'Hara in Gone With the Wind who said, 'After all, tomorrow is another day.' That saying is the only thing that got me through the rest of the day. Okay, enough from me, how about all of you? How were your days?"

"In a completely different vein, mine was similar to yours," John said. "I made the mistake of parking my Red Pony Food Truck in front of a large office building. I'm usually in that spot a couple of days a week. Wrong day to do it. I didn't know that one of the companies that has an office in the building had brought in all their sales managers from across the country. The manager of that particular office is one of my better customers. In fact, Max and I have catered a number of events at the office, as well as at his home.

"Anyway, he told everyone that he would buy lunch for them at The Red Pony Truck in front of the building. My bank deposit was hefty, but looking out the food truck window and seeing a line snake around the block in the blink of an eye, is not the best experience in the world. Particularly when you're not expecting it.

"Max and I have never worked so hard, and we ran out of everything. I mean, the last guy got a peanut butter and jelly sandwich. I tried to make it as gourmet as I could by slicing off the crusts and putting fried bananas on it, but I don't know if it helped. Sure would have appreciated the manager giving me a head's up on that one."

"John, after that experience, the last thing you need to do is cook for us. Why don't we all go into town, and I'll treat everyone to pizza," Laura said.

"Bite thy tongue, woman. What I need is comfort food and comfort is what you're getting for dinner. Meatloaf, mashed potatoes, and a killer chocolate chip cookie dough cheesecake. Nothing is better than comfort food at a time like this."

"I agree, John. In fact, just hearing what we're going to have is improving my mood. Thanks for the great timing," Jeff said. He turned and looked at Marty. "What's wrong? You look really glum."

"That's because I am. I'm sorry, Jeff, but I feel like I've really let you down. Miles Reed was a no-go as well."

"Wait a minute," Les said. "What do you mean as well? As well as what?"

Marty spent the next half hour relating her conversations with Priscilla, Eve, and Miles. When she was finished, she said, "That's about it except for Randy Miller. He's the last one on my suspect list, and given what Miles said, I'm sure Randy will have an alibi as well, actually, pretty much the same one Randy has. I would expect there would be security camera footage of him going in and out of his office building, condominium, and the restaurant where they had lunch which will corroborate his alibi."

"I was going to tell you that my friend in Las Vegas called me on the way here and confirmed what you're saying. Randy Miller is not the murderer, so I guess we're back to square one. Let's just let it go tonight, enjoy John's comfort food, and get a good night's sleep. I'm sure things will look better in the morning."

"Think that's my cue for dinner," John said. "All I need to do is fix the mashed potatoes. Max and I will be back in a minute."

Marty turned towards Laura and said, "Got any words of wisdom about now? I feel like I'm at a dead end, and I sure could use some help."

As she usually did when she was being asked for psychic advice or thoughts, Laura became quiet and closed her eyes, as if deep in thought. After a few minutes she said, "I told you about the mailbox and that turned out to be valid. I still don't know the meaning of the words, 'Act of Mercy', but I am getting something new. The words are superimposed over a cell phone. Does that mean anything to you?"

It was Marty's turn to be quiet. Finally, she said, "Not at all. I mean, everyone has a cell phone, so why would one be more important than any other? Are you getting anything else?"

"Sorry, Sis, not a thing. We'll just have to wait and see what it means. These things always become clear at some point in time."

"I know, but after today, my patience and ability to wait until something is clear has run out."

"The only other thing I'm getting is that it's almost over. I have no idea what that means, but at least it sounds positive."

"I agree," Marty said.

After they'd finished dinner and John and Jeff had helped themselves to seconds of everything, Max came out of John's house with the cheesecake. "This is the first time we've tried this. Hope you like it," he said as he sat down and began serving them.

"No, I don't like it," Jeff said. "I absolutely love it. This is one of the best things you've ever made. I mean who wouldn't like cheesecake on a chocolate chip cookie crust. Yes, thank you very much, I will have a second piece."

*****

"Jeff, I really am sorry," Marty said as they got ready for bed. "I was so sure it was one of them. They all had motives, but after today, I have no idea where to go with this."

"Nor do I, but we'll worry about it tomorrow. The good news is that at least the mayor's son's case is finished and other than dealing with some press people and finishing up some paperwork, I'll be free to work on the Joseph murder case. Get some sleep, Marty, and remember Scarlett's words, 'After all, tomorrow is another day.' Good night, love."

"Good night," she said, turning off the light and hoping that tomorrow would be the day the murder was solved, rather than just another day.

CHAPTER TWENTY-FIVE

The insistent ringing of Marty's cell phone on the nightstand next to the bed woke her out of a sound sleep. She was having a dream about Miles Reed performing in Las Vegas to a standing room only audience wearing the Elvis jacket Carl had taken to Jimmy Joseph's home on the day of the murder.

She was somewhat disoriented when she picked up her phone, noticing that Jeff's side of the bed was empty and that it was 7:00 a.m. "This is Marty," she said as she answered the phone in a groggy voice.

The voice on the other end was barely audible and Marty was sure whoever was calling was crying. "Hello, hello? Who is this?" she asked.

She heard sobbing and then a woman's voice said, "Marty, it's Ruby," was all she was able to get out before she started crying so hard, she had to stop talking.

"Ruby, what's wrong? Why are you calling?"

"It's Horace. Somethin's terrible wrong."

"Is he sick? Has something happened to him?" Marty asked.

"Yeah, he's got a bad case of the flu, but that ain't what's wrong," she said, still sobbing

"Then what's wrong?"

"It's horrible, jes' horrible. Ya' gotta' help me. I can't believe it," Ruby said.

"I'm sorry, Ruby, but I can't help you if I don't know what the problem is. What would you like me to do?"

"I need to talk to ya', but not at the house here. Could ya' meet me somewhere?"

"Certainly. When and where?" Marty asked.

"There's a Starbucks coffeeshop at 110 North Palm Canyon Drive. Can ya' meet me there?"

"Of course. I can be there in 45 minutes. Will that work for you?"

"Yeah, see ya' then."

Marty threw on some clothes, fed and walked the dogs, and put a leash on Patron. She didn't know what she was going to encounter, but having Patron with her seemed like a good idea, and she knew he'd be welcome at the outdoor seating at Starbucks.

"Okay, Patron, you're going with me. Duke, we'll be back…"

She was interrupted by Laura opening her door and calling to her. "Marty, I need to talk to you before you go see Ruby."

Marty thought about asking her how she knew she was on her way to see Ruby, but knowing Laura's psychic ability, figured it would be a waste of time.

"I just want you to know that it will be over today and be gentle."

"Wait a minute, Laura, that's all you've got for me?"

"Yes, that along with the words I told you about yesterday, 'Act of Mercy.' I don't know exactly what it means, but that's what I'm getting. It will all be over soon."

"Thanks for confusing me even more. I have no clue why Ruby needs to see me and no clue what any of this means, but if you're right, and based on past experience, you probably are, I'll tell you all about it tonight."

"Marty, you're not in any danger. You can leave Patron at home today."

"Are you sure? I promised Jeff I'd take Patron with me."

"Yes, I'm absolutely certain. See, he's not growling or showing any other signs that something is wrong. Anyway, it would probably be easier for you."

"Okay, Laura, thanks. See you later."

She took Patron's leash off, walked through the gate, got in her car, and began the drive down the mountain to Palm Springs and Ruby.

A little over a half hour later Marty walked by the Starbucks outdoor patio and saw Ruby sitting at a table, dabbing her eyes. Marty waved and indicated she'd be there in a minute. She'd left her house in a hurry, without having any coffee or eating, so a bagel and a cup of coffee were sorely needed before she talked to Ruby.

"Good morning, Ruby," she said as she sat down at the table where Ruby was sitting, wiping tears away from her face. "I'm sorry something is causing you so much pain. How can I help?"

"It's Horace…"

"Yes, you mentioned that when you called. What's wrong with

Horace?"

"He's got the flu, but that ain't why I called."

"All right, why don't you take a deep breath and then tell me what's troubling you?"

Ruby was quiet for several moments as she tried to gain control of herself and then she said, "He called out for me this mornin'. Our bedrooms are next door to each other. I went into his room and he said he was really sick and runnin' a high fever. I felt his forehead and he was very hot. I tol' him I'd get some aspirin and I went into his bathroom. I opened the medicine cabinet and, and, and…"

Ruby started sobbing again and couldn't continue speaking. Marty reached across the table and patted her hand. "It's okay, Ruby. Whatever it is, I'll do what I can to help."

"He's gonna' go to prison, ain't he?" Ruby asked, crying harder.

"Horace? For what?"

"For killin' Jimmy."

"Wait a minute, Ruby. You've lost me. I have no idea how you got from getting aspirin for Horace, because he was sick, to him going to prison. I need you to fill in the missing pieces."

Ruby took several deep breaths and began to speak rapidly, as if she was afraid if she didn't get the words out quickly, she'd never be able to say them.

"I opened the medicine cabinet in his bathroom and I saw a strange bottle in there. I took it out and looked at it. It was a powder called ricin. Think ya' said that was in the pellet that was shot into Jimmy's leg. And that's what killed him. Horace killed Jimmy."

It was Marty's turn to be quiet. She had no idea what to say.

"Ruby, I agree that finding the poison that was responsible for Jimmy's death in Horace's medicine cabinet doesn't look too good for him, but that doesn't mean he killed him."

"Mattera' fact, it does," Ruby said shaking her head up and down. "I also found the gun that shot the pellet. I gave Horace some aspirin and he fell asleep. While he was sleepin', I looked in his desk. The gun was in there as well as directions on how to make a ricin pellet that could be fired from a gun. Horace shot Jimmy with the pellet he'd made and now he's goin' to prison."

"Ruby, I don't know what to say. I agree with you, that it certainly looks like Horace was the one who shot him, but it makes no sense. They were very close, and from everything I've seen and understood, Horace worshipped him."

"He did, and that's why I can't unnerstand what happened. I felt if I told ya, maybe you could get yer' husband to help. If regular police found out, and I figured sooner or later they'd get around to searchin' Horace and my bedrooms, they'd just take him in right then and there and throw him in jail." She looked pleadingly at Marty. "Please help us."

"Ruby, if Horace was responsible for murdering Jimmy, as you well know, that's a serious crime. Maybe there was some reason for it. I think we need to talk to Horace, and I think my husband should be there. Do you mind if I call him?"

"No, please do. Tell him we need help."

Marty picked up her cell phone and went to Favorites. She pressed Jeff's name and a moment later heard his voice on the other end of the line. "Hi, sweetheart. Are you finally up? I had to leave early, and I didn't even have time to start coffee for you. Sorry."

Marty told Jeff everything that had happened and then said, "Ruby's still with me. What should we do now?"

Jeff was quiet for a moment and then he said, "You're in

downtown Palm Springs now, right?"

"Yes."

"Okay, meet me at the Joseph house in fifteen minutes. I just need to do one thing then I'll be on my way. As I remember, the house is gated. I would assume Ruby knows the gate code, but you better ask her."

Marty looked at Ruby and said, "Jeff wants to meet us at your house in fifteen minutes. He wants to make sure you have the gate code, so we can get in."

"Yeah, I know it."

"Jeff, she has it and we'll see you there in fifteen minutes."

CHAPTER TWENTY-SIX

Marty followed Ruby to the Joseph house and through the open gate. Jeff pulled in behind her. On the way over, Marty's mind was whirling. She couldn't make sense of what Ruby had told her. If Horace murdered Jimmy, what was his motive? They were as close as brothers, and he had an extremely good life. What reason could he possibly have for doing something like that?

She hoped against hope that Horace had a logical explanation for the ricin and the gun. It made no sense to her. Maybe Jeff could put the puzzle pieces together.

Marty introduced Ruby to Jeff as they walked up to the door of the house. Ruby had started tearing up again. "Ruby, here's how I would like to handle this," Jeff said. "I want to see how Horace is feeling. Maybe the aspirin reduced his fever, and he'd feel like talking to me."

"Will you be comin' into his room with me?" she asked.

"Yes, given what you've told Marty, I have no choice but to make sure that a police officer is with him. Unfortunately, until I find out something more, he definitely is our number one suspect, and I can't risk him trying to run away."

"Yeah, I was afraid of that. Let's go see him."

Jeff turned to Marty and said, "I'd like you to stay here in the hallway. Let me assess the situation, and since you know him, if it's feasible, I'd like you to join us. I'll call you if I think you should come in."

While she waited in the hallway, Marty heard voices coming from inside the room, then a few minutes later Jeff called for her to join them in Horace's bedroom. He was sitting up in bed with a questioning look on his face.

"Marty, why don't you sit down? I've told Horace I have a couple of questions I'd like to ask him in connection with the murder of Jimmy Joseph."

He turned to Horace and said, "Horace, Ruby called Marty this morning and asked to meet with her because she was very concerned about some things she found. Specifically, she found a bottle of the poison, ricin, in your medicine cabinet as well as an air gun type of pistol in your desk. What can you tell me about those things?"

Horace looked at Ruby and said, "Why, why would ya' tell anyone that you found those things?"

Ruby looked back at him and said tearfully, 'Horace, we both loved Jimmy like a brother and he loved us. I know you couldn't kill him. We was as close as three people could be. I jes' couldn't not say somethin' about findin' those things. I know there's got to be some logical reason, but I sure can't come up with one.

"I thought maybe since Marty knew us and how close the three of us were, it'd be better if her husband talked to you rather than some uniformed police officer who wouldn't care about us. Please, Horace, tell us some logical reason why you had them things. Please tell me ya' wasn't the one who killed my Jimmy."

Horace looked away from her and was quiet for several long moments. The room was utterly quiet and you could cut the tension in the room with a knife, as the three of them looked at Horace.

When he finally spoke, his voice was filled with emotion and he said, "Ruby, Jimmy loved ya' like a sister. Ya' know that. He knew the state you were in when he had his heart attack. What he didn't tell ya' was that he had terminal cancer. He was diagnosed when he was in the hospital recoverin'. He knew it would kill ya' to see him die day by day."

"Jimmy had cancer? Oh, no. Why didn't he tell me?"

"Jes' what I said. He knew it would kill ya'. He started beggin' me to do somethin' to end his life. He said he wasn't brave enough to take his own life and how would it look to his fans. I told him I didn't want no part of it, but he said I was the only one he could trust.

"One night when he was watchin' television, he saw some crime show about how a guy had killed someone by making a ricin pellet and shootin' it at his victim. The man died shortly thereafter. The day after he saw the show Jimmy told me that's what he wanted me to do. He also told me that he'd amended his trust to leave the bulk of his estate to you and me, includin' this house."

"Oh, Horace, no. You murdered him and he arranged for everythin' to be left to us. Wasn't he worried that ya' would be charged with murder and go to prison?"

"Yes. That's why he had his attorney draw up some paper that said in legal mumbo-jumbo, that Jimmy had asked me to kill him, and I was doin' it outta' love fer him. He told me to keep the paper as insurance in case somehow it was discovered I was the one who did what Jimmy called an Act of Mercy.

"He said he'd talked to his doctor and told him he wanted to invoke the right to die law, but he wasn't gonna' do it himself, he was havin' someone do it fer him. He said if someone found out that I did it, the doctor would testify that it was Jimmy's wish to die, and I was simply followin' his wishes."

"Horace, are you telling me you admit to killing Jimmy Joseph by shooting him with a pellet which contained ricin?" Jeff asked.

"Yes, sir, but I wouldn't call it a killin'. It was like Jimmy said, an Act of Mercy."

"Horace, I have no choice but to arrest you for the murder of Jimmy Joseph, and I have to tell you that this is probably the worst moment I've had in my career since I've been on the police force. Unfortunately, I have to do the job I have sworn to do, namely uphold the laws of the State of California,

Jeff then read Horace his Miranda Rights, reading off a card he carried in his wallet. When he'd finished he said, "Horace, I have a question. Why didn't Jimmy take a pill from a doctor once he'd decided to invoke the right to die law?"

Horace was quiet for several moments and then said, "Jimmy was real proud, sir, and he loved his fans. He didn't want his fans to think he'd do somethin' like that. He thought if it looked like he'd been murdered, it would be kinda' glamorous and all the entertainment media would pick it up and even in death, he'd still be a star. He didn't want his fans to see him as an old man who took a pill to die."

"Mr. Jeff. What's gonna' happen to Horace?" Ruby asked.

"I have to take him to the station and have him booked for the murder of Jimmy Joseph. He'll be there until he can get an attorney and post bail. If the two of you are going to inherit Jimmy's estate, and I rather imagine it will be large based on this house and what Marty has told me about his collection, I think it would be wise to hire the best criminal lawyer you can find. Obviously, you'll be able to afford it.

"No one can predict what judges and juries are going to do, but given what you've just told me, I find it hard to believe that either a jury or a judge would give Horace the maximum penalty for murder. With a good lawyer, and the doctor's statement, I would assume it would be a light sentence or best scenario, not serve any time and do community service. I rather doubt anyone could hear this story and not be touched.

"Ruby, would you show me where the bottle of ricin is and the gun? I'll need to take them with me as evidence. Horace, we need to go to the station. If you feel very sick, I'll get an ambulance to take you to the prison ward of the hospital, and we can do the paperwork there. If not, I'll personally take you to the station. Your call."

"Sir, I really don't feel good. I think maybe I better go to the hospital. Didn't want to worry Ruby none, but I ain't felt good fer the last coupla' days."

"Fine, I'll make a couple of calls. Give me a minute. Ruby, why don't you pack a little bag for Horace to take with him?"

"Yes, sir. Can I go with him?"

"I think it would be better if you drove to the hospital in your own car. That way you'll have some transportation when you want to leave."

Within thirty minutes Horace was transported to the hospital by ambulance, accompanied by two policemen Jeff had called to the scene.

After the ambulance left, Jeff turned to Marty and said, "The case is solved, but I sure am sorry it ended this way. Why don't you go home and take it easy for the rest of the day? If you feel as lousy as I do about this whole thing, I imagine you could use some rest. I won't be far behind. It's times like this when I wish I'd never chosen this profession."

"I understand, Jeff, but you had no choice. You weren't the one who made the decision. Jimmy did. See you at home."

*****

Marty couldn't keep from crying on the way home. To think that Horace might spend time in prison for doing what his best friend and almost brother had begged him to do seemed wrong. Particularly given the fact that Jimmy Joseph had terminal cancer and wouldn't have lived long anyway.

I don't understand why someone would ask their friend to do something that could cause them to go to prison, she thought. *He must have decided no one would ever discover the truth and that his murder was just a random act of violence. And to think it was done because he didn't want his fans to know the truth. He wanted to be glamorous even after death, but at what cost to Horace? This is just about the saddest thing I've ever heard.*

Marty pulled into the driveway and greeted the dogs. The compound was quiet, for which she was glad, given her state of mind. She had no desire to talk to anyone. The only thing she wanted to do was get in her house and have a good cry.

When she was finished crying, she fixed herself a sandwich and was sitting at the kitchen table thinking about the unfairness of things in life when her phone rang, the screen indicating it was a call from Jeff.

"Hi, Jeff. Did you get Horace taken care of? I have to tell you I came home and had a good cry. His explanation of why he did it was just about the saddest thing I've ever heard."

"Sweetheart, it's not going to get any better. There's no way to sugarcoat this. Horace just died in the hospital. He had a seizure and even though a team of medical personnel were present when it happened and did everything they could to save him, he died. The coroner happened to be in the hospital on another matter and immediately came up to his room.

"I told him what had happened and he said based on his handling of the ricin when he made the pellet used to kill Jimmy, he thought that Horace had probably died from ricin poisoning. If it doesn't go into the bloodstream immediately like Jimmy's did, it can take several days for death to occur. The coroner was pretty certain that's what happened to Horace."

"Oh, Jeff…" Marty started crying again and both ends of the phone were silent. Marty thought she heard Jeff choking back a lump in his throat as well. Finally, she composed herself enough to say, "Well, maybe it's for the best. At least he didn't have to be the target of some media circus and go through a trial. Was Ruby with him?"

"No, she came to the hospital, and after he was taken to his room and seemed to be in reasonable spirits, she said she was going home to get his iPad and some other things he'd probably want. It wasn't pretty, so I'm glad that won't be her last memory of him. I drove over to her home and told her in person."

"How did she take it?"

"As I'd expect. She was devastated. First Jimmy is murdered, then she finds out her brother is the murderer, and then he dies by the same poison he used to kill Jimmy. You couldn't script that. I asked her if she had someone she could call to be with her and she gave me her sister's name. She's flying in and will be here tonight. I'm having one of my men meet her at the airport and take her to Ruby's home. This really has to be about the saddest case I've ever been on."

"Oh, Jeff, I'm just devastated. Horace was really such a nice man and Ruby's a wonderful woman. I wonder what the future will hold for her?"

"I have no idea, but I doubt she'll be staying in that house. I wouldn't be surprised if she left Palm Springs. Too many bad memories. I have to go, Marty. See you in a little while."

"Loves."

EPILOGUE

Two months later, Jeff called Marty and said, "I just got a phone call from Ruby and I thought you'd want to hear how she's doing."

"Very much. How is she?"

"She seems to be doing well. She bought a home in Tupelo and feels good that she moved back there after Horace's death. She said to tell you hello and thank you for arranging for the sale of the memorabilia collection."

"With a lot of help from Carl."

"I know that, but she's crediting you with it. Anyway, with the proceeds from the collection and the sale of the house, she's set for life. The only thing I regret is that I wasn't able to keep the press at bay in some fashion. I'm glad I no longer have to read about Horace's death and Jimmy's murder."

"Me too. As much as I hated the amount of coverage the press gave it, I do understand. Plus, I've heard that one of the studios is thinking about making a movie out of it," Marty said.

"That's probably true because Ruby told me she'd been approached by a studio asking her if she'd consider being a consultant if they got the funding to make the movie. She said she didn't want to revisit all of the pain, but maybe if she was a consultant, the movie would reflect the truth, rather than the rumors that Horace and Jimmy were involved. She said there was absolutely no truth to it, but it was the type of story the news loved."

"Jeff, I just had a thought. If the movie is made, I wonder if they'd have an appraiser and a detective in it, and if so, who do you think the director would choose to play us? Maybe they'd even want us to play ourselves."

"Marty, I don't see that happening, so you can forget about having your name on a star imbedded in cement on a sidewalk in Hollywood. See you later."

RECIPES

BEEF STEW

Ingredients:
1 tbsp. olive oil
3-4 lbs. beef chuck roast, cubed into 1" pieces
1 white onion, chopped
1 cup baby carrots, cut into bite size diagonal pieces (If you don't want to cut them yourself, they're available in the packaged salad area of your supermarket)
2 stalks celery, chopped in small pieces
18 oz. can whole tomatoes, cut into chunk size (If you wish, you can add some of the juice from the can.)
1 tsp. salt
1 tbsp. ground pepper
4 garlic cloves, minced
1/3 cup tomato paste
5 cups beef broth (I use "Better Than Bouillon.")
1 cup red wine
1 tbsp. Worcestershire sauce
1 tsp. dried thyme
1 lb. baby potatoes, part halved & part chunked
1 ½ cups small brown mushrooms (If you use larger ones, quarter them.)
1 cup frozen petite peas, thawed
2 large slices sourdough bread, lightly toasted, then torn into bite

size pieces
1 tbsp. corn starch (to make slurry & thicken stew to taste)
Wondra flour, as needed (I use it to thicken stew to desired consistency)

Directions:

Use a sharp fileting knife and cut roast into bite sized 1" sized cubes. Cut around fat & gristle and discard. In a large Dutch oven (or pot), over medium heat, add olive oil & cook all sides of beef cubes until seared, about 10 minutes.

You'll probably have to do this in two batches, so you don't crowd the meat. Transfer beef to a plate and set aside. In the same pot, cook onion, carrots, and celery until soft, 5 minutes. Season with salt and pepper. Add garlic and tomato paste and cook until garlic is fragrant and tomato paste has darkened, about 2 minutes.

Place beef back into Dutch oven, then add broth, wine, Worcestershire sauce, thyme, and chopped whole tomatoes. Bring to a boil. Reduce heat to a simmer. Season w/salt & pepper to taste. (I like to go heavy on the pepper). Cover and simmer for 30 minutes.

Add potatoes and simmer, covered until potatoes are almost tender, about 15 minutes. Add peas, mushrooms and bread pieces and continue to simmer for 7-10 minutes, stirring as necessary. If you want the stew to be thicker, add the corn starch slurry, half at a time, as needed. For even more thickness, sprinkle a small amount of Wondra flour on top of stew mixture. Allow to cook for 1 minute, and then stir into the stew. Enjoy!

Note: Recipe makes 6 servings. I like to serve it in large soup bowls with Irish soda bread. Great for dunking in the stew. Enjoy!

DEVILISH DECADENT CHOCOLATE COOKIES

Ingredients:

16 oz. semisweet chocolate, chopped

½ cup butter
¾ cup all-purpose flour
½ tsp. baking powder
½ tsp. salt
4 jumbo eggs
1 ½ cups sugar
2 tbsp. instant espresso powder
1 tbsp. vanilla extract (Don't use imitation. It makes a difference.)
2 cups fine quality bittersweet (56%-60% cacao) chocolate chips
2 cups walnuts, coarsely chopped

Directions:
Heat oven to 325 degrees. Line 4 cookie sheets with parchment paper. In a large heavy-bottom saucepan, melt the semisweet chocolate and the butter over medium-low heat until smooth, about 5 – 7 minutes, stirring occasionally.

In a medium bowl whisk the flour, baking powder, and salt together. In a large bowl beat together the eggs, sugar, espresso powder, and vanilla until mixed and slightly foamy. Beat in the chocolate mixture and then the flour mixture. Stir in the bittersweet chocolate chips and the walnuts.

Using about 2 heaping tablespoons of dough for each cookie, spoon the dough onto the cookie sheets. Bake until the cookies are cracked on top and moist in the center (don't overbake because you want the cookies to have a fudgy center.) Transfer the cookie sheets to a baking rack and cool completely before removing. Enjoy!

COD FISH WITH LEMON CAPER SAUCE

Ingredients:
1 lb. skinless cod filets, ½ inch thick, patted dry
2 tbsp. olive oil
¼ tsp. kosher salt
¼ tsp. fresh ground pepper
2 medium size lemons, juiced (You can substitute limes.)

¼ cup capers, drained
3 tbsp. unsalted butter
3 cloves garlic, mashed
2 tbsp. flour (I prefer Wondra flour for coating & dusting.)

Directions:
Heat oil in large frying pan until oil is shimmering. Meanwhile, lightly dredge cod fillets in flour so they are barely covered, then sprinkle salt & pepper on the fillets. Flip over and repeat the process on the other side of the fillets. Add the cod fillets to the pan and cook until golden-brown on each side. About 3 minutes per side.

Remove fillets to a plate and cover with foil to keep warm. Drain off half of the oil remaining in the pan. Increase the heat to medium-high and add the lemon juice. When it begins to bubble add the capers, butter, and garlic and swirl over the heat until the butter is completely melted, about 1 minute. Thicken the sauce as needed with a shake or two of Wondra flour. Spoon the sauce over the fish and serve immediately.

Note: This recipe serves 4. Best to buy frozen cod fish in package containing individually vacuum-packed cod filets.

BRUSSEL SPROUTS WITH SWEET PARMESAN CHEESE SAUCE

Ingredients:
1 package of Brussel sprouts or loose (approx. 15-18)
2 tbsp. vegetable oil
1 tbsp. sugar
2 tbsp. white vinegar
Salt & freshly ground pepper to taste
5 tbsp. grated Parmesan cheese

Directions:
Heat oven to 350 degrees. Cut the bottom off of each Brussel sprout, peel off the outer leaves, and cut each one in half,

lengthwise. Scatter the halved Brussels in an ovenproof glass pan. Sprinkle 2 tbsp. water over the Brussels, cover with plastic wrap, punch 3-4 holes in the plastic wrap, and heat in microwave for 4-5 minutes on high until nearly tender.

Meanwhile, mix together the oil, sugar, vinegar, salt, and pepper in a small dish. When Brussels are finished in the microwave, remove from microwave and pour the oil/sugar mixture over the Brussels and place in oven for 20 minutes. Five minutes before they're finished, sprinkle Parmesan cheese over the Brussels and continue to bake. Serve & enjoy!

CHOCOLATE CHIP CHEESECAKE

Ingredients:
1 pkg refrigerated chocolate chip cookie dough
16 oz. cream cheese, softened
¾ cup sugar
1/3 cup whipping cream
1/3 cup sour cream
Cooking spray
2 tbsp. chocolate syrup for drizzling on top

Directions:
Preheat oven to 350 degrees. Spray 9" springform pan with cooking spray. Form 6 cookies from the dough and place in the freezer.

Press cookie dough into the bottom of the pan. In a large bowl, beat the cream cheese and sugar with an electric mixer until smooth. Add the eggs, one at a time, beating and scraping the sides of the bowl after each addition. Beat in the whipping cream and the sour cream. Pour filling evenly over the cookie dough. Crumble the frozen cookies over the filling.

Bake 55-60 minutes or until set around the edge and the center is almost set, but still a little jiggly. Turn oven off and leave door ajar.

Leave the cheesecake in the oven for an additional 30 minutes. Remove cheesecake from oven. Run a metal spatula around side of pan to loosen. Refrigerate cheesecake for 2 hours or until well chilled.

Remove sides of pan. Serve and enjoy!

Paperbacks & Ebooks for FREE

Go to www.dianneharman.com/freepaperback.html and get your FREE copies of Dianne's books and favorite recipes immediately by signing up for her newsletter.

Once you've signed up for her newsletter you're eligible to win three paperbacks. One lucky winner is picked every week. Hurry before the offer ends!

ABOUT THE AUTHOR

Dianne lives in Huntington Beach, California, with her husband, Tom, a former California State Senator, and her boxer dog, Kelly. Her passions are cooking, reading, and dogs, so whenever she has a little free time, you can either find her in the kitchen, playing with Kelly in the back yard, or curled up with the latest book she's reading.

Her award winning books include:

Cedar Bay Cozy Mystery Series

Cedar Bay Cozy Mystery Series - Boxed Set

Liz Lucas Cozy Mystery Series

Liz Lucas Cozy Mystery Series - Boxed Set

High Desert Cozy Mystery Series

High Desert Cozy Mystery Series - Boxed Set

Northwest Cozy Mystery Series

Northwest Cozy Mystery Series - Boxed Set

Midwest Cozy Mystery Series

Midwest Cozy Mystery Series - Boxed Set

Jack Trout Cozy Mystery Series

Cottonwood Springs Cozy Mysteries

Coyote Series

Midlife Journey Series

Red Zero Series

Black Dot Series

Newsletter

If you would like to be notified of her latest releases please go to www.dianneharman.com and sign up for her newsletter.

Website: www.dianneharman.com,
Blog: www.dianneharman.com/blog
Email: dianne@dianneharman.com

PUBLISHING 5/10/19

CAROL

BOOK THREE OF

THE MIDLIFE JOURNEY SERIES

https://amzn.to/2UxR9dm

Letting go of a lifetime of hurts isn't easy. It's pretty hard to believe that Happy Ever After even exists.

Can Carol let go of the past and move on to the future with a handsome chef whose intentions towards her are an open book? It's pretty clear to everyone but Carol that he's in love with her. It's also pretty clear to everyone that Carol has some issues she needs to overcome before she can take the first step to midlife happiness.

A Maltese puppy and good friends who conspire with the chef just might make everything possible. But then again, whoever said life will go smoothly and just the way you want it to was wrong.

This is the third book in the Midlife Journey Series by a two-time USA Today Bestselling Author. The series highlights women who have a second chance at happiness after having dealt with life issues that happen to all of us by the time we're in our midlife years.

Open your smartphone, point and shoot at the QR code below. You will be taken to Amazon where you can pre-order 'Carol'.

(Download the QR code app onto your smartphone from the iTunes or Google Play store in order to read the QR code below.)

57395094R00088

Made in the USA
Columbia, SC
08 May 2019